*For Jude
and for Lara:
You know what you did.*

Prelude

The End of Summer

The moon rose high in the sky.

Rylie's veins pulsed with its power. It pressed against her bones, strained against her muscles, and fought to erupt from her flesh.

A wolf's howl broke the silence of the night. It called to her, telling her to change. "No," she whimpered, digging fingernails into her shins hard enough to draw blood. "*No.*"

Rylie burned. The fire was going to consume her.

The moon called her name, but it would be the end of her humanity if she obeyed it. She would never see her family again. She would never see her friends or graduate high school. Rylie might not die, but her life would be over.

Yet if she didn't change, the boy she loved would die at the jaws of the one who changed her.

Rylie had to lose him or lose her entire life. But was love worth becoming a monster?

One

Full Moon

Three months earlier.

Empty buses idled in the parking lot at the bottom of Gray Mountain. Almost everyone had arrived for the first day of camp an hour ago, but one girl came in her own car.

"This is it," announced Rylie's dad. "Camp Silver Brook." He tried to sound upbeat. Rylie could tell he was faking it.

She glared at the camp's entrance. The footpath was marked by a tall sign carved out of a tree, but she couldn't see any cabins from the parking lot. Dense trees prevented sunlight from reaching the ground even though the day was sunny, so the forest looked dreary and dark.

Three months of this: dirt, pine needles, and having to share a cabin with strangers.

"Thanks for the ride, Dad." Rylie didn't pretend to sound happy. Missing the bus hadn't been an accident.

"Come on, it's not that bad. Aren't you excited? You can ride horses and go in a canoe and take lots of hikes." Her dad got to the trunk before she could pick up her bag.

"Yeah. I'm thrilled. Can I have my backpack?"

"Let me walk you in," he said.

Rylie grimaced. "*Dad*. I'm almost sixteen. I don't need to be babysat."

"Come on, humor your old man."

She rolled her eyes but didn't argue.

They walked up the trail together, backpack slung over his shoulder and her gaze fixed on her pristine leather hiking boots. Rylie's mom said the shoes were a going away present for the summer, but she knew they were actually an apology for the divorce.

The buses pulled away by the time Rylie and her dad reached the top of the hill, leaving their car alone at the bottom.

After living in the city for so long, the forest seemed too quiet. Her footsteps echoed against the slopes of the mountain and her breath was loud in her ears, although it might have been the asthma making her wheeze. Rylie touched her pocket to reassure herself that the inhaler was there. She was probably allergic to everything in the woods.

It was a long walk up the trail on Gray Mountain. Rylie's dad wasn't in good shape, and he was struggling within minutes. "Look, Rylie," he panted, and she recognized the beginning of another apology.

"Don't worry about it," she interrupted. "Really."

He scrubbed a hand over his balding scalp, wiping the sweat away. "It will all be better by the time you come home in August. I promise."

She didn't reply. What was there to say? It wouldn't be better in August. It would never be better unless she could go back to a house with her mom and her dad. A house where they didn't yell all the time. A house where they didn't get rid of their daughter so their lawyers could fight in peace.

Rylie heard voices before she saw the other campers: four large groups of girls, all around her age. They laughed and chatted, pushing each other around, meeting old friends and making new ones. Counselors with clipboards led them toward a fork in the path marked by a sign indicating "Silver Brook." The other sign read "Golden Lake."

"Excuse me," said Rylie's dad. "Excuse me!"

People turned to look at them, and Rylie stared harder at her shoes. A counselor broke away from the group. "You must be Rylie! Glad you made it!"

"Thanks," she told the ground.

The counselor scanned her clipboard. "Let me see... there you are. Group B."

Rylie's dad slung an arm around her shoulders in a half-hug. She tried to inch away from him. "Do I need to check her in?"

"No, but it looks like her paperwork isn't finished. Did you mail it in?"

"Uh... I might have forgotten," he said.

Hope swelled within her. Maybe he hadn't finished Rylie's enrollment and she wouldn't be able to stay. She could walk back down the hill, get in the car, go home, and pretend this camp thing didn't almost happen.

"That's okay," the counselor said. Rylie peeked at her name badge. Louise. She looked like a high school gym teacher. "You want to come to camp and fill a couple things out?"

And all hope was gone.

"Sure!" he boomed. "Good day for a hike!" Rylie could have withered and died on the spot.

Louise clapped her hands. "All right, campers! Let's catch up with the others!"

Rylie trailed behind the girls in Group B. They all wore short-shorts and fake tans. One had a gold chain around her ankle with a single diamond, and Rylie glimpsed perfect white teeth when she talked.

Many of the people in Group B were from Rylie's city, but they went to the private school, May Allan. Rylie's parents would have sent her there if it wasn't so far from home. Seeing her potential classmates made her glad. Rylie was the richest kid at school, but she would have been nothing at May Allan.

It was a long hike to the girls' cabins, and Rylie was worried her dad would have a heart attack before they made it. Louise set a fast pace to catch up with the other groups. He barely managed to keep up.

Once they reached the camp, Louise directed them to a log building overlooking the lake. "That's the office. I need to take Group B to their cabins."

"I could just go home with you, dad," Rylie said in a last-ditch effort to escape.

He laughed, bracing his hands against his knees to catch his breath. He seemed to think she was joking. "The paperwork will only take a minute, pumpkin. Why don't you wait out here?"

She sat on one of the benches, smoothing her hair down with her hands. There was already a canoe out on the lake. Rylie could just make out more cabins on the other shore—probably the boys' camp. She had read about Camp Golden Lake in the brochure. The boys and girls weren't allowed to hang out at all.

Rylie studied the rest of her surroundings from the bench, digging the toes of her hiking boots into the dirt. The common area was unremarkable. They had cut down trees to make seats around an amphitheater with a fire pit in the middle. Rylie could see the recreation hall and the dining room, and paths leading to cabins elsewhere in the camp.

It was oppressively quiet, like she was the only thing alive in the woods.

"Three months," she mumbled.

What in the world was there to do in a forest for three months? Walk around? Look at trees? Commune with the stupid deer? At least in the city, there were libraries and coffee shops. There was nothing like that here. Rylie wasn't even sure there were showers.

A splashing sound drew her attention back to the lake. The canoe had drawn close to her side of the shore. Rylie shielded her eyes to look at the person sitting inside.

It was a boy. He was probably her age, or maybe a little older, judging by the breadth of his shoulders. His arms were dark brown, like he had already been camping for months, and he was looking right at her.

Rylie chewed her bottom lip. One of the guys from Golden Lake? He was going to get in trouble if he was caught so close to their shore.

She raised a hand to wave at him. After a moment, he waved back.

Her dad came out of the office. "Okay, everything is settled. They told me you're in Cabin B3. Sounds like you'll be with some nice kids! Why don't I take you there?"

"I can find it myself," Rylie started to say, but her dad looked sad. She rolled her eyes. "Yeah, sure. Show me." Glancing back at the lake, she saw the canoe had moved on. The boy was gone.

The cabins for Group B were laid out in a rough circle around another fire pit. A few girls were trying to get a fire going, carrying wood up the path and piling pine needles between the rocks. The sun was still high, but Rylie could tell sunset would fall quickly in the mountains.

"Here it is!" her dad said. He rubbed his hands together, looking between Rylie and the cabin like he wasn't ready to let her go. "I could help you unpack if you want."

"I really think I can handle it," Rylie said.

He sighed and handed the bag over. "You're right. I have to let you go someday."

"You could let me go home," she whispered, but he didn't hear. He hesitated at the mouth of camp.

"Love you, pumpkin," he called. Someone near the fire giggled.

Rylie slung her backpack over her shoulder. "Love you too, dad." She didn't wait for him to leave. She couldn't stand to see the other girls whispering.

It was going to be a very long three months.

•〇•

Rylie managed to skip orientation by telling Louise that she was sick. Once she was alone, Rylie pulled out her diary and opened it to the first blank page.

Dear diary, she wrote. *I hate my life.* Rylie considered the words with a frown, chewing on her pen cap. *Camp could be interesting, I guess. Maybe if I see it as a learning thing instead of a punishment for the divorce...?*

She dropped her pen. Why fake optimism?

Stretching her cell phone over her head, she searched for reception in the cabin's tiny loft. No bars. She wouldn't even be able to text her friends back home. Rylie flung her phone to the bed and tried not to let frustration choke her.

"I can't believe this," she told the empty room.

Rylie hid from a few campfire sing-alongs and hikes in the first week, but after begging illness for a few days, Louise forced her to go to the infirmary.

She tried to fake a cough. The nurse wasn't fooled.

"You can stay overnight, but you're going back to the cabins tomorrow."

"Are you sure?" Rylie asked. "I could be diseased and contagious. Maybe I should go home."

The nurse gave her a look which obviously meant *nice try,* and Rylie was back in her cabin the next morning.

She didn't mind sleeping on a tiny cot in the loft. (All the other beds were taken by the time she got there.) She did, however, mind having to share her living space with a bunch of teenage girls.

Rylie's friends back home were mostly guys, since all the girls she knew were catty and stupid. And these ones hated Rylie for no reason at all.

They shot nasty looks at her before going to the morning activities, and they didn't talk when they saw her in the evenings. Her roommates avoided her during the day and treated her like an alien when Louise forced them to interact.

Dinners were the worst. The cooks offered some kind of meat product slathered in gravy on most nights, and just looking at it made her queasy. Rylie had been a vegetarian ever since she learned how animals were butchered in the seventh grade.

"Tofu?" asked the man in the hairnet behind the counter. "You want *tofu?*" Which meant, of course, they didn't have it.

She sat down to eat her carrot sticks, trying to imagine herself anywhere but the mess hall: maybe watching a movie at the second-run theater on thirty-third street, writing a journal entry on a park bench, or reading a book at the coffee shop on the corner.

Rylie closed her eyes and let her imagination carry her away. There were no moths fluttering around the lights and no mosquitoes. Only percolating coffee and an indie guitarist in the corner. Maybe a cute guy at the next table. She could sip a mug of chai tea and drift away on guitar melodies.

"Where is *she* from?" whispered a girl at the table behind her, stirring Rylie from her fantasies. She was loud enough for everyone to hear. It had to be deliberate.

Another piped up in the same fake whisper. "I don't know. Her dad dropped her off. He was wearing glasses like this." Rylie glanced over in time to see the girl holding her hands in front of her eyes to indicate big circles. "And he was super fat."

"Where's she been all week?"

"She hides in one of the cabins. She *never* comes out. It's so freaking weird."

"Look at her clothes."

"Look at her *hair*."

Rylie's cheeks flamed as she touched her white-blonde hair. Even though she always thought it was too pale for her face, she had never heard anyone talk about her like that before. A rope of embarrassment twisted in her stomach.

She dumped her remaining food into a trash can and hurried back to camp. Sunset cast long shadows over the path. Rylie wanted to be back in bed before it got dark so she could hide from the night's campfire activities.

The cabin's lights were already on, and the sounds of laughter poured out the window. Rylie pushed the door open.

Her four roommates were clustered around a cot by the door. "...but I hope he doesn't ask me out," read Patricia in a nasal voice. "I don't want to reject him and hurt his feelings, but I don't want to be his girlfriend, either."

Rylie recognized those words. She had written them herself.

In her diary.

The contents of her backpack were spread across the room as her roommates pawed through them. Patricia held out her diary so everyone could see it. None of them had noticed Rylie yet.

"I bet she made it all up," said Kim. "Who would want to go out with *her*, huh? She wouldn't even show up for the date!"

"What are you doing?"

The girl with the gold anklet looked up. Amber. She was holding a pair of Rylie's shorts in one hand and Byron the Destructor, her favorite stuffed cat, in the other. "We noticed you hadn't unpacked yet. We were just... helping," she said before bursting into giggles. The other girls followed suit.

Rylie stared at them. Her embarrassment in the mess was nothing in comparison to the numbness spreading through her now.

"Nice teddy bear," said Kim before dissolving into snickers.

"You guys—you—I can't..." She didn't know what to say. Her mouth worked, but no sounds came out. "It's not a bear. It's a *cat*."

She ripped the backpack off the bed. They had gone through everything—even her underwear. Rylie snatched her diary out of Patricia's hands.

"Way to be grateful," laughed Amber. "Didn't you hear me? We were helping!"

Eyes stinging, Rylie backed up until she hit the door. Why were they laughing? What was so funny? "Of course," she whispered hoarsely. *Helping.*

Rylie flew out of the cabin and passed Louise, who was setting pokers and marshmallows on a table by the fire.

"Where are you going?" called Louise. "Rylie? Rylie!"

She ran without looking where she was going. She passed a line of people heading back from the dining hall, and she knew they could all see her crying. Everyone would know what Patricia and Amber did to her. The teasing would only get worse.

Rylie had to stop by the office on the shore of the glistening lake. Her chest felt constricted and she wheezed with every breath. She fumbled for her inhaler and tried to let all the air out of her lungs, but it took a few tries before she could calm down enough to breathe at all.

She sucked down the medication. Wheezed again. Took another puff. Slowly, her air passage relaxed.

"How could they do this to me?" Rylie rasped, fist clutched around her inhaler. "I hate them. I *hate* them." The full moon's reflection blurred in the water. It was laughing at her too, just like everyone else at the camp.

She couldn't stand to be there a minute longer. Rylie threw her backpack onto her shoulder and plunged into the forest.

She didn't know how long she walked. The trail grew thinner and twistier. She stumbled over a log in her path and the bark scraped her shin. Blinded by tears, Rylie pushed on. She didn't know if it was the way back to the parking lot, but it didn't matter since she didn't have a way home. She needed to get *away*.

The trees grew so close together that she had to climb over them to keep going. Occasionally, she glimpsed the full moon between the branches, but she could always feel it watching her.

At long last, Rylie came to a cluster of trees she couldn't pass. Too tired to find a way around them, she flung herself onto a mossy boulder to rest.

Her racing heart gradually slowed. All the fury and embarrassment drained out of her, leaving only a small, burning coal of shame in the pit of her belly.

None of this had been in Rylie's plans. She wanted to go to a summer concert series at the park by her house. She planned on seeing a new exhibit at the art museum, too. Maybe it wasn't glamorous, but that was how she liked to have fun: on her own in the city, or with a couple friends from school. Not surrounded by harpies at camp.

Of course, now Rylie wasn't surrounded by anyone. She had gotten her wish. She was alone.

She was also lost.

Rylie looked around from her perch on the boulder, but there was no sign of a path now, much less humanity. She didn't even have any light. Fear trickled in at the edges of her mind. She had no maps, no compass, or anything else to help her get around.

Rylie pulled out her cell phone. Still no reception. The GPS didn't even work.

Something rustled in the bushes nearby. She froze.

"Hello?"

She lifted her cell phone to illuminate her surroundings with the screen. It cast stark shadows on the bushes and trees, but it was too dim to see further than a couple feet.

The soft, rhythmic sound of feet against pine needles whispered around her.

"Who's there?" she called. Fear made her throat tighten again, and she gripped her inhaler. Rylie crept around a tree, peering into the darkness. Maybe it was a deer or something. "If that's you, Amber, you better hope I don't find you. I'll— I'll beat you up!" She sounded much braver than she felt.

A bush shook behind her. Rylie turned, but nothing was there.

Her breathing roared in her ears like an ocean tide. The entire forest was silent and eerie, as though everything living had vanished. Even the moon was gone now.

Picking a random direction, Rylie started walking, keeping an uneasy eye on the trees around her. She wished she had a flashlight. Even better, she wished for a helicopter so she could fly off the mountain.

She eased around a thick tree. A pair of golden lights flashed in front of her.

Eyes.

Rylie jumped backward, but the lights disappeared instantly. She froze. Her heart pounded.

The eyes had been low to the ground, more like an animal than a human. She could hear it rustling amongst the foliage.

She was being stalked.

Lifting her cell phone a little higher, she stared around for another glimpse of eyes. A twig cracked like a gunshot. Rylie gasped and spun, and her inhaler dropped from her hands.

She bent down to search for it, but her fingers only found dirt and pine needles. Her heart pounded. Her lungs started to ache.

Something growled, and Rylie decided she didn't care about her inhaler anymore.

Backtracking toward the trail, she whispered a silent prayer to the black sky: "Please, *please* just let me get out of here. I'll never do anything this stupid again. I swear."

A hulking gray body flashed in front of her. She jerked back and her heel caught a low rock. Rylie lost her footing. Her cell phone flew from her grip. The back popped off, the battery dislodged, and all light vanished.

She hit the ground. Something heavy, hot, and furry struck her body.

Pain ripped across Rylie's chest. She screamed into the night, but nobody was there to hear her.

Two

The Boy

Daybreak.

Rylie flung a hand over her face to shield her eyes from the sudden sunlight. How could she have forgotten to close the curtains in her bedroom before falling asleep? Dragging the sheets over her head, she rolled over and tried to go back to sleep.

"Campers! Turn out!"

Campers?

It took a long moment for her thoughts to fall into order, but then she remembered everything: her dad abandoning her at camp, her week in hiding, the horrible dinner, finding the girls looking through her belongings, her flight into the forest...

And the attack.

Gasping, she sat up. Rylie was on her tiny cot in the loft, but she had no idea how she had gotten there, much less survived the beast.

"What the...?"

She took inventory of her body. Her arms and legs were fine. Her stomach and chest—why did she remember so much pain in her chest?—were unmarked. She ran her fingers over her face and found nothing. The window by her bed was open to the cool morning air.

Had everything in the forest been a nightmare? It felt so real: the eyes, the furry gray body, the dense trees and dark night.

But how would she have gotten back? Rylie had been hopelessly lost.

She reached under her cot for her backpack and found nothing there. Her other belongings were missing, too. Her clothes, her journal, and her cell phone were nowhere in sight. She must have dropped it all in the forest.

"Stupid, stupid, stupid," Rylie muttered.

The other girls were getting out of bed to go to the showers. Amber shot a glance up at the loft. "What a freak," she hissed to Patricia.

Rylie was already too upset to care about the insult. Her roommates filed out carrying toothbrushes and towels and shampoo, and she sat on her cot feeling just as lost as she had the night before.

Louise poked her head through the cabin doorway. "Come on," she said. "You can't stay inside all day. If you're feeling good enough to run off in the middle of the night, you're feeling good enough to shower."

"But..."

"Yes?"

"I can't find any of my stuff," Rylie said. "My backpack. My clothes."

Louise planted her hands on her hips. "You took them with you last night when you left camp. Did you drop them on the trail?"

"I don't know."

"Tell me where you went and I'll look for you."

"I don't know," Rylie repeated. When the counselor gave her an incredulous look, she added, "It was dark." *And I don't even remember how I got back.*

"I'll tell the other counselors to watch for your bag. In the meantime, I'll get clothes and a towel so you can shower."

She followed Louise to the office. The woods around camp were so much more alive than the day before. Birds sang in the trees, building nests and swooping after bugs. Chipmunks scurried up and down tree trunks while rabbits burrowed through the underbrush. The earthy, woodsy scent of dirt and cinnamon bark filled her nostrils.

Louise found clothing and a towel for Rylie. "These are unclaimed items from last year's lost and found," she said. "You can keep them. Get going."

Rylie tried to suppress her disgust at the idea of secondhand clothes, but if she hoped to start blending in with the other girls, this wasn't the way to do it. Baggy t-shirts and too-large shorts were going to make her look shrunken, awkward, and an even better target for teasing.

The water for the showers was pumped from the brook, so it was freezing cold. She rinsed off quickly and emerged shivering, wrapping the ratty old towel around her body. Rylie stared down her reflection in front of the mirror. Her blonde hair lay limply around her face and shoulders, and her wide eyes looked helpless and prey-like.

She watched everyone leave through the mirror. Several girls whispered and pointed as they passed, but her reflection distracted her before she could get upset.

Four parallel, silvery gashes had appeared on her chest, like old scars. But Rylie didn't have any scars.

She turned this way and that until the light caught her skin in such a way that she could make out the lines. They looked like claw marks. "It doesn't make sense," she murmured. Someone behind her giggled, and Rylie's cheeks grew hot. She hadn't meant to speak aloud.

Dressing quickly to hide the scars, she went to the dining room alone. At least there had to be *something* vegetarian for breakfast, like pancakes or toast.

The forest during the day felt like a completely different world than the forest at night. An early morning sprinkling of rain left lush moss and dewy sparkles on the bushes. Golden sunlight made shadows dance on the trail.

Rylie was so absorbed in the life and colors of the woods that she didn't notice she had company until he stepped in front of her. It was the boy from the canoe.

"Hey, hang on a second!"

His voice was deeper than she expected. Seeing him closer than before made her realize he wasn't just dark-skinned and broad-shouldered—he was also *really* cute. He had a strong nose and full lips, offset by shaggy brown hair slanting over one eye. A single fang hung from his pierced left ear.

"Hi," she said, her cheeks growing hot. "Are you from the boy's camp?"

He gave her a long look up and down, face to feet, like he was sizing her up. "My name is Seth."

"I'm Rylie. I don't think you should be here."

Seth reached into his back pocket and pulled out a slender book with a pen tucked in the pages. "Is this yours?"

She snatched it from his hands. "My journal! Where did you find that?"

Rylie flipped through the pages, afraid something would be missing, but everything looked intact. The corners were a little dirty, and there was a deep gash across the cover, but it was otherwise fine.

"I was hiking out past the boy's camp and found it by the trail."

"Was there anything else? An inhaler? A backpack?"

"I didn't see anything," he said. His dark eyes burned right through her. Rylie wished she could turn invisible so he wouldn't see her in the clothes from the lost and found. "Are you okay?"

The question startled her so much that Rylie responded honestly. "No."

"Why?"

"I don't know," she said. Rylie meant to leave it at that, but once she started it talking, she couldn't stop. It all came spilling out at once. "I hate it here. My parents dumped me off so they could forget about me for the summer. The other girls tease me, and I didn't do anything to deserve it. All my stuff is gone and I think I'm going crazy. Plus, I *hate* the outdoors."

The corners of his mouth twitched. "Sorry."

She flushed. "But it's better now I have my journal."

"Good." Voices approached. It sounded like one of the other groups had finished showering and was going to breakfast. "I should go. I'll see you later."

"Thanks for my journal," she said, but he had already vanished.

The archery range was set up in a field by the lake. Louise ignored Rylie's complaints of a stomach ache and made her come along, but didn't try to make her participate. Rylie sat on a bench facing the water and tried to make out the boy's camp on the other side.

"Bull's eye!" crowed Amber. Her little group of friends laughed and high-fived in congratulations. Rylie shot her a nasty look before returning her attention to the water.

There were no canoes today. No sign of Seth at all. She wanted to see him again, even though thinking about him was enough to make her blush. How had he known the journal was hers?

Pulling her journal out of her pocket, Rylie gazed across the water. She chewed on the end of her pen while she decided what to say. She couldn't begin to describe her hazy memories of the previous night, nor could she explain her mysterious new scars. And all that was shadowed by the urge to write about Seth and his stunning eyes.

She prepared to write, but Rylie froze before she could lay pen to paper. Her last entry wasn't the only thing on the open page.

A line had been written at the bottom in sharp, slanted handwriting which didn't belong to her. Rylie was mortified at the thought of Seth reading her journal until she read what he had written:

Be careful. You're in danger now.

Three

Observations

Dear diary,

I ran into the boy from the lake yesterday. He left me a warning: "You're in danger now." What does it mean? I need to find him again. I need to know what he knows.

Something is definitely happening. There are weird scars on my chest, and I don't know if I dreamed the animal attack or not.

I can't think straight. I feel weird.

Anyway, I've resigned myself to being stuck at camp for the summer. I won't say I'm happy, because I'm not. Most of my time is still spent avoiding the other campers. But occasionally, I do find ways to have fun...

"What are you doing?"

Rylie looked up at the sound of Louise's voice. She was sitting behind her cabin, digging the blade of a knife into a tree growing too close to the back wall. The other girls were swimming in the lake, but Rylie drew the line at hand-me-down swimsuits. Instead, she decided to leave her mark on the forest.

She had been daydreaming and hadn't paid attention to what she carved into the tree trunk. Rylie looked at it now. It was a stick figure of Amber—a very dead Amber.

Louise held out a hand. Rylie gave her the knife. She had stolen it from the kitchen when she went to beg the cook for more vegetarian options.

"What is that?" Louise asked, indicating the carving.

"I don't know."

Rylie got up to go back into the cabin. The counselor followed.

"Why don't we talk for a minute? Do you mind?" She sat on the steps and gestured for Rylie to do the same.

"What do you want?"

"I know you're having a hard time, Rylie," Louise said. "Your dad told me about what's happening at home. We just want you to be happy. Are you having a good time?"

"No," Rylie said.

Louise squeezed her shoulder. "You may not want to hear this from me, but you're not going to have fun unless you let yourself have fun. How many activities have you participated in here?"

She focused on her hiking boots, no longer so new and clean. "None."

"Do you enjoy anything? Swimming? Arts and crafts? Horseback riding?"

"I like horses," Rylie told the ground.

"Okay, how about this? Group B doesn't have horseback riding on the schedule for a few days, but I can send you along with another group this afternoon. Would you like that?"

She considered the offer, nudging a clump of dirt over an ant hill. The bugs scattered. Getting away from Amber and Patricia to ride horses sounded better than anything else she had done so far. "I'll try it."

"Great! I'll talk to the other counselors."

Louise was as good as her word. That afternoon, someone from Group D showed up to walk Rylie to their camp, where nobody recognized her as the weird girl who hid in her cabin for a week. No one even gave her a second look.

The counselor, Samantha, clapped her hands to get the attention of all the girls in the group. "All right, everyone. Line up single file!"

"This is stupid," someone muttered nearby.

Surprised, Rylie turned to see who had spoken. It was a short, sullen, dark-haired girl wearing full-length jeans and a sweater. She looked impervious to the heat. Black ink covered her hands and wrists with drawings of her own design.

"What's stupid?" Rylie asked.

"Lining up like we're cattle," the girl said. "They tell us to obey and we jump to do it."

Her mouth twitched in a half-smile. "It is kind of sadistic, huh?"

"Nice to know someone gets it. I'm Cassidy."

"Rylie."

"Where did you come from?" Cassidy asked.

"Group B." Rylie searched for an explanation as to her temporary change in groups, but she didn't think it would be smart to admit everyone in her group hated her. Instead, she said, "I wanted to ride horses."

Cassidy nodded. "Cool."

When the line formed and moved out, they stood together. Neither spoke. Rylie enjoyed the companionable silence of having connected with someone, anyone, for a brief moment—even if it was a girl who seemed to be as miserable as she was.

"You from the city?" Rylie asked after awhile.

Cassidy nodded. "North end. You?"

"East side, around the art district."

"I go there a lot. It's pretty cool. I want to be a comic book artist." She pushed her sleeves up to her elbows to show off her arms. "There isn't enough for me to draw on here, and not enough time for me to do it anyway. They're all about the stupid outdoors. I've had to go on a hike every day."

"I know what you mean," Rylie said. "If I eat one more charred marshmallow, I'll go nuts."

"It's always like that. This is my second year."

"Why did you come back if it's this bad?"

She rolled her eyes. "Parents."

Rylie let Cassidy walk in front of her so she could check out her arms. Some of the drawings were really good. All the characters had wide, bright eyes and big lips. She had inked the moon on the back of one hand, surrounded by trees and what looked like a bear.

"Here we go," Cassidy muttered when they finally reached the stables. The horses were tethered to hitching posts in anticipation of their ride for the day. They were already saddled up and ready to go. Rylie was almost excited. *Almost.*

She didn't listen to the instructor's explanation of how to mount and ride safely, nor did she pay attention to the description of the trail. Rylie had been riding a hundred times before, so she didn't need a safety talk.

It seemed like hours before they let the girls get on the horses. "What's wrong?" Rylie asked when Cassidy refused to mount.

"I don't like horses."

"My aunt has horses at her ranch in Colorado. I can help you. I know what I'm doing." Rylie approached her horse confidently, reaching for its bridle. The horse's eyes widened, showing the whites all around the iris, and it blew hard through the nose. "Uh... I *think* I know what I'm doing."

Tentatively reaching for the reins again, the horse backed up until its tether went tight. It shied from her hand, nostrils flaring and ears pricking.

The wind shifted subtly, and the other horses grew uncomfortable too. Rylie lunged for the bridle.

The horse shrieked and reared. A heavy hoof struck her in the collarbone, and she fell with a cry, trying to shield her face.

"Everyone get away!" shouted a stable hand.

Rylie tried to crawl away from the rain of stomping feet. Her shoulder was white hot. Fire pulsed through her veins with every heartbeat. The horse whinnied and screamed, eyes rolling.

A hoof landed right next to her head. Rylie scrambled away quickly on all fours, and Cassidy grabbed her arm to haul her to her feet. She staggered, knees buckling.

"Oh my God! Are you okay?"

"My shoulder," Rylie groaned.

Samantha pushed Cassidy aside to look at Rylie. "What happened? You, over there! Go get the nurse!"

"No, wait," Rylie said, touching her shoulder. The fire had subsided and her pain vanished with it. "Never mind. I'm... fine."

"You were kicked. Your collarbone must be broken!"

Rylie fingered the bone gently, probing where it had hurt. There wasn't even a tender spot anymore.

"I guess it missed me. I must have fallen over."

Samantha didn't look like she believed her. "The nurse needs to look at you. Can you walk?" She led Rylie away, and Cassidy flashed a smile as she passed.

"That was wicked," she whispered.

Rylie smiled. She actually smiled.

The nurse couldn't find anything wrong, but insisted on keeping her for a few hours anyway. Rylie pulled out her journal and perched on the end of a hospital cot by the window.

A bird landed on the windowsill before flitting away. She watched it disappear into the sky.

I spooked a horse today, diary, and it kicked me. I'm sure it broke my shoulder, but I walked away unmarked. Something is happening to me.

I have to go back. I'm going to retrace my footsteps and find out where I went on the full moon. Maybe all my answers are hiding out there in the forest.

I don't know what it is, diary. I'm starting to feel like a completely different person...

Four

Hiking

Rylie waited for a chance to get away, but Louise watched her closer than ever after the horse incident. She never managed to be alone anymore, whether it meant getting walked to the showers, mess hall, or back to the cabin at the end of the day.

It took two days for the opportunity to arrive.

"All right, campers," Louise called. Rylie looked up from her journal. She sat on the cabin stairs while everyone else chatted around the morning campfire. "Put on an old pair of shoes, because we're going creek-walking this morning!"

Rylie grimaced. She had brought old shoes with her, but they vanished with everything else in her backpack. She would either have to wear hand-me-downs or go barefoot, and neither sounded appealing.

She bowed her head over her journal and went back to writing, hoping Louise wouldn't notice her, but the counselor came to stand by her immediately. "When I say 'campers,' that does include you, Rylie."

"I don't have shoes," she said without looking up.

"Shoes are optional. Come on, you'll like it."

"As much as I liked horseback riding?"

"You're hilarious. Come on."

Rylie snapped her journal shut. "Fine."

The brook did look silver in the sparkling sunlight. Louise took them to a shallow part of the stream, where natural dams made the water quiet and slow, and most of the girls jumped right in without being invited. Rylie found a large rock and climbed on top, watching everyone else with her journal in her lap.

Louise handed out packets, which had an illustration of a river and beavers on the first page. Rylie took one. It was entitled "The River Habitat." She rolled her eyes and dropped it off the back of the boulder.

"Naturally dammed streams, like this area, provide a safe haven for many creatures," Louise said. "This is the home of all kinds of things, like fish, water fowl, and frogs. If you open up your packet, you'll see a list of animals living in this habitat. We're going to play wildlife bingo while creek walking."

"I'll pass," Rylie muttered.

She didn't feel like writing, so she took a blank page from the back of her journal and started doodling. Rylie let her mind wander. Her pen trailed from the top of the paper to the bottom, and from side to side, and it started turning into a picture—a drawing of a wolf prowling around a cabin.

Rylie studied her illustration. It wasn't very good. Unlike Cassidy, she wasn't much of an artist.

Someone screamed. She turned, sharp eyes immediately falling on Patricia, who was on all fours in the water.

Louise hurried forward. "What happened?"

"My ankle!" she wailed. "I think my ankle broke!"

The counselor helped her up. "I'll take you to the infirmary," she said, pulling Patricia's arm over her shoulder. "I'll be right back. Amber, will you keep an eye on everyone until I return?"

"Of *course*," Amber said, visibly preening over the new responsibility.

Louise and Patricia limped toward camp, and Rylie saw her chance to escape. She tucked her journal in her pocket, counted to ten, and then set off after them.

"Where are you going?" Amber demanded.

"Away," Rylie said.

"Louise left me in charge. I say you have to stay."

She snorted. "Yeah. Right. I'll do that."

Amber yelled after her while she trotted down the trail, but her voice faded quickly. "I'll tell Louise! You'll be in big trouble!"

"Such big trouble they might send me home," Rylie said, knowing Amber couldn't hear her anymore.

There was no way to tell where she had gone on the night of the full moon, so Rylie retraced her tracks to the lake. It was the last place she could clearly remember. She kept an eye out for Louise and stuck to the sides of the trail so she wouldn't accidentally cross paths with anyone.

Once she reached the lake, she picked a direction and kept going. Rylie knew she wanted to escape Camp Silver Brook, so she selected the trail leading higher on Gray Mountain. It was as far from camp as possible.

She walked for a long time. The shadows of the trees lengthened and the trail started to disappear. Even though it had only been a week since her flight into the forest, she wasn't nearly as worn out by the hike as before. Maybe camp was good for her fitness after all.

After what felt like ages, she began to feel déjà vu. Something was familiar, even though she couldn't remember ever having been there before.

Rylie searched the ground between the thick trees, spreading bushes and peeking between rocks. It had been moist the other night, and she saw a couple dents in the dried mud that might have been her footprints. She stepped next to one of them to compare her boot to the size of the indentation.

Something shiny glinted near her foot. Her phone!

She scooped it up and was pleased to find it was only a little dirty, even though it wouldn't turn on. The battery was missing. She pocketed it, dropped to her knees, and kept searching.

The battery and the back of the case were only a couple feet away. Rylie reassembled her phone, but the battery was dead. Since the cord was in her backpack, she wouldn't be able to charge it until she went home and used the spare.

Although her backpack was nowhere to be seen, she did locate Byron the Destructor behind a rock. "There you are," she said fondly, brushing a couple of ants off his forehead.

Her phone and stuffed cat hadn't made it so far on their own. How had she gotten back to camp by morning?

She gazed around at the surrounding forest. One of the trees looked strange. There were gashes in the bark like deep, parallel knife cuts. Or claw marks.

Rylie touched the silvery scars on her chest. Claws.

"What are you doing here?"

A man approached from amongst the trees. He was overwhelmingly tall and broad, like a brick wall come to life. He had angry, slanted eyes and a Camp Golden Lake t-shirt. His yellow hair was shorn close to the scalp.

"I dropped my phone on a hike the other day," she said, holding up the pieces to illustrate.

"Hiking? Out here?" he demanded, eyes flashing.

Rylie started to shrink back, but something deep within her consciousness told her to stand her ground. "Is that a problem?"

"Girls aren't allowed on the Golden Lake side of the mountain. What group are you in?"

"Group B."

He yanked her back onto the trail by the elbow. Rylie tried to shake him off, but his grip was like an iron shackle. "Don't you know better than to wander off alone?"

"I guess not," she said. "Let go of me!"

His hand tightened in response. He marched her back to Camp Silver Brook. His stride was much longer than hers, so it was hard to keep up. She kept stumbling.

"Slow down!" Rylie demanded, squirming.

"No."

He took her straight to the Group B campsite, navigating Silver Brook with the expertise of someone who had been there before. Louise nearly collapsed with relief when she saw Rylie. "Thank God!" she said. "Are you okay? Where did you go?"

"I found her on the other side of the lake." He finally released Rylie's arm, and she rubbed her elbow. She could still feel his fingers digging into her skin.

"You found her on—oh Rylie, what were you doing over there?"

"I was looking for my backpack."

"I'm so sorry, Jericho," Louise said. "I'll take care of this. Thanks for bringing her back."

"I'll see you around, Rylie," he said Something about the way Jericho pronounced her name sent chills down her spine.

Rylie followed Louise into the cabin and sat on the edge of her bed when the counselor pointed. "The usual punishment for crossing over to Camp Golden Lake is confinement to your cabin and restriction from activities for a few days, but that wouldn't work on you, would it?"

"You can confine me if you want," she said.

"That's what I thought." Louise shut her eyes and massaged her temples. Rylie got the impression she was silently counting to ten. "Tell me the truth. Are you planning on running off again?"

"No," she said honestly. What good would it do? She wouldn't find her clothing or the rest of her belongings if she went back to search a dozen times. The forest was too thick.

"What am I going to do with you?" Louise asked. Rylie shrugged. "Fine. Stay here for the rest of the day. Did you at least find what you hoped you would find?"

"I guess."

She left, and Rylie curled up on her bed to gaze out the loft window. Everyone else was in the middle of their afternoon activities, and she was grateful to be alone with her thoughts.

Someone stood out amongst the trees. She sat up to get a better look. It was a boy with dark hair, wide shoulders, and a black tank top—Seth. Rylie leaped off her cot and hurried down the ladder, racing around the side of the cabin.

"Seth! I need to talk to you!"

But he was nowhere to be seen.

Five

New Moon

A few days later, Group B was assigned another round of archery. The afternoon was perfect for it. A cool breeze carried cool air down the mountain and the sky was slightly overcast so that the sun didn't get in their eyes. Louise gave Rylie an encouraging smile when she lined up to take wrist and finger guards like everyone else.

Picking out her equipment, Rylie moved aside to watch everyone else string their bows. Louise wedged one end of the staff between her feet and forced the other into a curve, hooking the string over the end. The bows resisted being bent. It looked difficult.

Rylie hooked the end of the string over one side, braced the bow between her hiking boots, and used all her strength to push down.

It shattered.

The loud crack made everyone look over at her. Rylie stared at the fragments of wood in her hand.

"What happened?" Louise asked, hurrying over.

"I don't know. It broke."

"The wood must have been rotten," she said. "You're not hurt, are you?"

Rylie shook her head and the counselor left to dispose of the fragments. She selected a different bow. This time, she bent it gently, and it gave easily under her weight. She slipped the string into place.

She gave a few test draws without putting an arrow on the string. It pulled smoothly. Rylie felt like she could have drawn the string back far enough to snap this bow, too, if only her arms had been long enough.

She got at the back of the line and waited her turn to fire at the hay targets. Since she strung her bow so much faster than everyone else, she was one of the first to shoot. Rylie mimicked Kim at the next target down, pointing her left arm straight out to the side of her body and aiming down her fist.

"Good, Rylie," Louise said encouragingly as she passed.

Patricia and Amber were whispering two lines away. Rylie shouldn't have been able to make out what they were saying, but their voices rang out crystal-clear in her ears.

"Have you seen what Rylie is wearing?" Amber whispered to Patricia. "She looks like a horse in drag with those skinny legs and that face."

Rylie glanced down at her clothing. She had tried to make the best of a bad situation and picked a bright red shirt out of the lost and found, coordinating it with a loose skirt. It didn't match her hiking boots, but she had no alternatives.

Her hand clenched on the bow. They shouldn't have talked badly about someone holding a weapon.

"Did you hear she tried to sneak off to the boy's camp the other day?"

"Yeah. She's so desperate for action. It's sick."

Anger made her vision blur. Rylie felt hot all over. She reached for her inhaler, recognizing the signs of an impending attack, but it wasn't in her pocket. It took her a minute to remember she had dropped it in the forest on the night of the full moon.

"Your turn," said the archery instructor, and Rylie stepped up to accept her arrows.

Her throat didn't close up. She didn't need her inhaler. But she needed to do *something* with her anger.

Patricia went to the front of her own line. Rylie felt the weight of eyes on her back, and she turned to see Amber watching her. She was wearing sandals and toying with the gold anklet with her toes. When she noticed Rylie looking, she pretended to be paying attention to Patricia instead.

"Loser," Amber whispered in a sing-song voice.

"Do you need help?" asked the instructor.

Rylie shook her head and got into position. She aimed carefully. She had never shot a bow before, but she felt confident and powerful. Rylie could do anything.

She pulled back on the string and released it.

Amber yelled, "Miss!"

Rylie's arrow whistled through the air and hit the tree behind the target.

"Miss Louise!" Amber finished. Patricia snorted. She had done it on purpose to make Rylie blow the shot.

"Yes?" the counselor asked.

Patricia engaged her in a conversation, gesturing toward the targets. Rylie heard Amber repeat, "Loser!"

Rylie turned until Amber was in the line of her bow sight. It would be easy to release the string and watch the arrow bury in her neck. She was confident she could make the shot from this distance.

"Hey! Bow toward target!" snapped the archery instructor.

She hesitated. It would be so easy...

But now Rylie was being watched, so there was no way to do it without being seen. She eased up on the string and aimed at the hay. Loser? Yeah, right.

Her second arrow flew true. It sunk deep into the yellow ring around the bull's eye.

After finishing, Rylie returned to the back of the line. Patricia still had Louise's attention, so Rylie approached Amber. "What do *you* want?" Amber asked.

Rylie folded her arms. "If you have a problem with me, you need to say it."

"What? You're crazy."

"You made me miss the target on purpose!"

Amber gave a barking laugh. "It's not my fault you suck at everything!"

"Why do you hate me so much?" she demanded.

"Oh, I don't know. Maybe because you're a freak who hides out in my cabin and wears nasty old clothing?"

Louise heard them. She started to walk over.

"At least I'm not an idiot who thinks my daddy's money makes me better than everyone else!"

"Shut up, bitch!" Amber pushed her, and sudden fury choked Rylie.

"Do *not* touch me," she said.

"Like this?" She planted both hands on Rylie's shoulders and shoved.

Something inside of her snapped.

Rylie slashed at the other girl's face with her fingernails. Amber shrieked and fell back.

She pounced on Amber and flailed with both fists. She wanted to beat her. She wanted to *hurt* her. But something about punching didn't feel right, like her hands weren't meant for that purpose.

She wanted to bite and tear.

Amber sobbed. It only made Rylie angrier, and in a way... hungry.

Hands clamped down on Rylie's arms and hauled her off Amber. She kept trying to hit and kick with a guttural roar. Rylie's skin was a thousand degrees. She was burning in her own fury.

It took Louise and two other girls to separate them. The moment they managed to get Rylie to her feet, however, Amber came flying at her. She lifted a hand to strike Rylie. "You're such a freak!" she shrieked.

"Cut it out!" Louise snapped, putting herself between them. "Your nose is bleeding, Miss Richmond. Take yourself to the infirmary. Now!"

Amber wiped the blood off her lip. Her her face paled when she saw it. "Freak," she spat one more time before flouncing away.

Louise rounded on Rylie.

"I have been very, *very* patient with you. My parents divorced when I was your age, and I went through a rebellious phase, too. But between your disregard for authority and aggressive behavior, we're reaching a breaking point. Do you understand?"

Rylie barely registered the words. She couldn't focus. Her flesh was overheating, and she could barely breathe. It wasn't asthma this time.

She shook her head to clear it, but it only made the world spin more. She could hear the chattering of squirrels and the birds in the trees and smell nearby deer scat. Her back legs didn't want to support her weight. It was all she could do to focus on Louise's moving mouth through the haze.

"Are you even *listening*?"

"I hear you," Rylie said, but the words felt clumsy in her mouth. It was too bright. She needed to go somewhere quiet, safe, and dark.

"Turn in your wrist guards and go back to camp. We'll talk later."

Rylie peeled off her protective gear and dropped them in the bucket. She glanced up at the sun. It was late afternoon, and it would be dark in a couple hours. For some reason, that felt very, very important.

She thought sitting down might make her feel better, but when Rylie planted herself on a bench around the fire pit to write in her journal, she found she couldn't stay seated. She kept shaking her head as she paced around the camp. A distant, persistent buzzing rattled in the back of her skull.

The sun dropped. It was getting dark. The new moon would rise soon, and it would be the darkest night of camp yet.

Her group didn't go to the mess for dinner. They roasted hot dogs and corn over the fire, and still Rylie paced. She had to move. She had to *go*. The dark trees were calling to her, and the muscles in her legs twitched like she was ready to run.

When they were done eating, the counselor let the girls build the fire higher and higher. The leaping flames licked at the starry sky. Ash drifted through the air and stung Rylie's eyes.

The heat from her anger had never faded, and now it settled in Rylie's bones. She thought she might be sick. "Can I go to bed?" she asked Louise in a hoarse whisper.

Louise looked annoyed until she caught sight of Rylie's pallor. Her lips drew into a frown. "Yes. Of course."

Rylie shivered hard as she crawled into her cot. She writhed in bed, rolling and twisting from side to side, and she struggled to keep lunch in her stomach.

The forest wanted her.

Shoving her window open, Rylie gasped cool air into her lungs. There was only one thing to keep her from dying of this fever, and she knew exactly what it was—running up the mountain and never stopping. She had to do it.

But Rylie couldn't afford being seen leaving again. She waited as patiently as she could in bed, too hot under the covers but too cold without them. She kept kicking them off and pulling them back on again.

All the other girls came to bed after awhile, but Amber wasn't with them. She had no sense of time anymore. She stifled her groans on her fist and in her pillow.

Peeking through the cabin door, Louise did a head count, and Rylie made sure she was visible. Her entire body shuddered with her efforts to stay still.

"Good night, ladies," Louise said with a pointed look in the direction of the loft.

She turned off the lights and shut the door. The girls immediately started talking. Rylie waited, feeling like she was going to crawl out of her skin. Little ants marched up and down her spine.

Eventually, the other girls fell silent. Their breaths grew deep. Everyone was asleep.

Everyone but Rylie.

Pushing the window open the rest of the way, she slithered through the small opening and dropped to the ground outside. She eased around the corner of the cabin, watching for counselors. They chatted outside their own cabin, holding mugs of hot tea and discussing problem campers—more specifically, Rylie and Amber.

"I just don't know what I'm going to do with her. Amber's parents are threatening to sue. Mr. Gresham's lawyer has already sent us a letter." Louise sighed. "I can reassign them to different cabins, but what good would that do? They go out of their way to get into fights." Rylie was tempted to stay and listen, but her body demanded movement.

She plunged into the forest, letting the fever drive her onward.

It was so much easier now. She never had to slow down to dodge the trees or leap over rocks. Her instincts guided her deeper and deeper into the wilderness. She could smell other beasts: wolves and bears, deer and groundhogs and squirrels. Rylie could even smell summer rain approaching.

Her lungs heaved with exertion. Her feet ached. Rylie's ribs ached like something was trying to burst out of her chest. A wolf howled in the distant night.

She collapsed to her knees. The fever had been momentarily cooled by her flight in the forest but returned with a fury, and Rylie tore at her own skin. She wanted to shed it like clothing. She wanted to let the thing inside of her out.

Throwing her head back, Rylie screamed.

The sound that ripped from her throat was more beast than human.

Rylie awoke just before dawn feeling cold and damp from dew.

She sat up with a groan, cradling her head in her hands. Rylie was amongst a mess of torn trees. A couple of the towering pines were snapped in half with their shattered pieces jutting toward the sky. Others were clawed like the grove where she found her cell phone. It looked like a storm had whipped through the clearing.

And that wasn't all. The ground had long claw marks in it, too. She ran her hands through the deep furrows in the ground and felt chilled when she saw that her fingers fit perfectly.

Rylie turned her fingers around to study her fingernails. They were caked with dirt and blood.

"What the...?"

Her head throbbed, and she pressed the heel of one hand against her temple. Thinking too much was hard, especially after the disorientation of finding herself in such a mess. A single thought emerged from her muddied brain: if she didn't get back to her cabin before Louise came to wake everyone up, she was going to be in big trouble.

Rylie had an easy time finding her way back. Even though she felt like she was recovering from the flu, the forest wasn't as maze-like as it used to be. She smelled breakfast and followed it.

The door to the counselor's cabin opened when she approached, and Louise emerged, muffling a deep yawn behind a hand. She went to the first cabin on the left. Rylie's was on the other end. She had enough time to sneak in— barely.

She scaled the cabin wall, using the grooves between the logs to lever herself up to the loft window. She wiggled inside.

Nobody else was awake yet. Patricia was snoring. Rylie had just climbed into the cot and pulled the sheets to her shoulders when Louise opened the door. "Good morning, campers! Shower time!"

Hoping she would be ignored if she stayed quiet, Rylie rolled over and pulled the blankets over her head.

"You too, Miss Gresham," Louise called.

Rylie picked out a fresh outfit and climbed down the ladder, trying not to grumble too loudly. Every inch of her hurt. She desperately wanted sleep, even though she felt like she must have been passed out most of the night.

Stretching under the spray of river water helped work the kinks out of her muscles, but it didn't clear her head. It felt like her skull was stuffed with cotton.

Drying off with another hand-me-down towel, Rylie dressed and went to the mirrors to brush the knots from her hair. She found several pine needles and a soggy caterpillar tangled up in the back. She tossed them in the trash and hoped nobody noticed.

Another group filed into the bathroom. Rylie caught sight of someone she recognized.

"Cassidy!"

"Hey," Cassidy said. She looked almost as beat as Rylie. Her head tilted to the side, and she gave Rylie a funny look. "You look different today."

Her heart sped up. "Really? What do you mean?"

"I dunno," she said. "But you're looking good. I need a shower wicked bad, but there's a big campfire thing this weekend. Songs or stories or something. I'll see you there, right?"

She nodded mutely, and Rylie fled to the mirror as soon as Cassidy turned her back. She studied herself closely, half-expecting to see fangs or fur or something equally horrifying.

Rylie didn't see anything other than the same silvery scar she'd had for two weeks. Then again, there was something a little off about her face. It wasn't quite the same reflection she had seen for the last fifteen years. She leaned close to the mirror. Her eyes had always been pale blue to match her pale blonde hair, making her washed out and ghostlike.

But her eyes were no longer blue.

They weren't quite brown, either. Instead, ribbons of deep gold veined the blue, like cracks in a sheet of ice. Rylie recognized that shade of gold. She had seen that color staring at her in the darkness of the forest two weeks ago when she was attacked.

Be careful. You're in danger now.

Rylie needed to talk to Seth.

Six

Solutions

Rylie didn't get the chance to catch up on her sleep that morning, nor did she get to search for Seth. She stumbled through breakfast and the morning hike. She barely kept her eyes open through the buffet line at lunch. She didn't even notice when Louise came to stand beside her.

"Do you see that?"

"See what?" Rylie asked, muffling a yawn.

"Tofu. I put in a special request for you," Louise said. There was indeed a small container of tofu next to the salad. It looked like nobody else had touched it. "And one other thing—I sent a letter to your parents explaining that you lost your backpack, so your mother sent a care package. I put it on your bed."

Louise left, and Rylie took several pieces of tofu. She was kind of excited. Having vegetarian food meant she might be able to finally satiate this gnawing hunger that had been growing within her for days. Nothing else seemed to make it better.

She went searching for a quiet table and passed by the entrees in the buffet. Folds of roast beef for sandwiches caught her eye, and Rylie hesitated. It looked good. *Really* good.

Revolted, Rylie sat down without taking any. What was she thinking? She hadn't liked meat in years.

She changed into her own clothes before heading to the recreation hall for arts and crafts, which was supervised by a counselor who wasn't familiar with Rylie's antics. She complained of sickness and was allowed to sit in the corner. It wasn't a lie this time. She laid her head down on the table and shut her eyes.

The back door of the recreation hall creaked open and a head with shaggy black hair poked in to look around. When his eyes fell on Rylie, he gestured for her to come outside. It was Seth again.

Rylie hurried over and slipped out the door. "What are you doing here?"

"I came to talk to you," he said. "Are you okay? You look terrible."

She tried not to feel stung by his insult. Even if she was exhausted, she wasn't in hand-me-downs anymore, and Rylie thought she looked pretty good. "I didn't sleep last night. Where have you been?"

"I've been around."

"Were you the one who wrote in my journal?" Rylie asked. Seth responded with a small smile, so she pushed on. "What did you mean? Why am I in danger?"

"You haven't figured it out yet? Do you know what happened last night?"

She faltered. "I told you I didn't sleep."

"Yeah? And how did you feel yesterday?"

Rylie started to lie. She wanted to tell him everything was fine and that it had been a normal day. But Seth's eyes were knowing. He would have seen right through her. "I was angry," she said.

SM Reine

"That's what I was afraid of." He took his bag off his shoulder to shift through it.

"What do you mean? What's happening to me?"

"Look at this," Seth said, handing her a book from his backpack. "I found this in the counselor library on my side of camp."

Rylie opened it to the bookmarked page. A large illustration of a half-man, half-wolf beast covered the left page. Its arms and legs were like a human's, but it had long claws, a shaggy mane, and a snout with sharp teeth. The full moon hung over its head. All the phases were drawn around the edges of page until it became a black new moon at the base.

When colonists first attempted to settle Gray Mountain, they found no natives to disturb. Instead, they were met with resistance from the forest itself as the animals fought to repel them. After years of battling, the forest spirits imbued a curse upon the mortals that cruelly slaughtered them: the uncontrollable ability to transform into a monstrous wolf at the apex and nadir of the moon.

Rylie shivered even though the day was warm. "Is this serious?"

"It's a book of legends," Seth said.

"So it's not true." She turned it over to look at the cover, which was plain green with gold trim. It looked serious enough.

"Who said legends aren't true? This mountain is holy for animal spirits, like Mount Olympus for the Greek gods. You've got the curse. You must have gone into the wild on the full moon."

"That's crazy," Rylie said. "I'm not a werewolf."

"Not *yet*," he corrected. "Haven't you been feeling strange? Like your senses are keener? Are prey animals more afraid of you?"

"No," she said stubbornly, but she couldn't help considering what Seth suggested. It would explain the horses. It would also explain why she craved red meat. "Why should I trust you?"

"Because I'm the only one who knows what's going on," Seth said. "There have been attacks before, so I knew you were in danger."

"Oh yeah? And how do you know that?"

"Like I said, I was doing some reading. I think these camps were originally built to guard Gray Mountain. There were never meant to be kids here."

"Then we should tell someone," Rylie said. "We should clear out the camps."

"Who would believe us?" Seth laughed. "Even you don't."

She bit her lower lip. "No, I believe it. Look at this." Glancing around to make sure nobody could see them behind the building, Rylie pulled aside the neck of her shirt to show him the scars. "They appeared after the full moon."

His laughter faded. "That looks bad."

"Yeah, I know. But why do you care?"

"Let's go for a walk," Seth said.

Rylie nodded. She wouldn't risk letting Seth out of her sight. Who knew when she would see him again?

Somehow, the horror of what Seth was trying to tell her seemed to recede a million miles away when they snuck down to the lake, dodging hikers and staff on the way. They slid down the boulders to reach the narrow shore where nobody could see them and walked along the sand.

Seth spoke before Rylie could start asking questions again. "So where are you from?"

"The city. I've lived there my whole life."

"I can tell. You're not much for the outdoors." He scooped a round, flat rock off the sand and bounced it in his hand, seeming to judge the weight.

"Not really," Rylie admitted. "But I'm starting to like it more. It kind of feels like I'm home here."

"Are you sure that's you talking?"

She ducked her head. "I'm not sure of very much anymore."

He whipped the rock out across the water. It skipped on the surface of the lake four times before sinking. They stopped to watch the spreading ripples.

"There are more books at the camp library," Seth said. "It sounds like it takes the curse a few moons to really settle in, so you'll have a couple weeks or months before you become a wolf. Until then, you should have partial transformations."

"You actually believe this stuff? Legends and werewolves? That's crazy," Rylie said.

"I guess I'm a crazy guy."

She took the diary out of her pocket, running her hand over the scratched cover. "How did you know this was mine?"

"I didn't. I was guessing. You look like the type."

"And what type is that?" Rylie asked.

Seth flashed a grin at her. "Beautiful."

Her cheeks got hot all over again, and Rylie pushed a lock of hair behind her ear as she tried to suppress a smile. "It sounds like you're dodging the question to me."

"Maybe. They're going to notice you're gone soon, so you should go back. What are you doing after lights out on Thursday?"

"Sleeping," Rylie said.

"Meet me down here," Seth said. "I'll see if I can get my hands on more books for you. There must be something we can do about this werewolf stuff."

"That sounds good." She felt light-headed. It wasn't a date, but she couldn't seem to convince her nerves of that. "I want to see the books myself. Will you bring them?"

"I don't think I can get them out."

"Then I'll go to the library," Rylie said.

His grin widened. "You're more trouble than you look. Okay. We'll go over together Thursday night."

Seth started to walk across the beach, but she called out to stop him. "You never told me why you're helping me!"

"I said I'm a crazy guy, didn't I?" He laughed and broke into a jog.

Rylie watched him disappear before returning the recreation hall, a smile stuck to her face. Nobody noticed she didn't have the same lanyards and milk carton candles as everyone else when they left.

Amber and her vicious clique kept talking about her at dinner, but Rylie barely registered it. She didn't care anymore. Her head was swimming with visions of Seth—their walk around the lake, his slanted smile, the way his muscles flexed when he skipped the rock across the water.

He was cute. *Very* cute.

But she was scared, too. She touched the faint ridges of scarring on her shoulders. Was she really going to become a monster?

She was grateful to find the cabin empty when she got back that evening. Rylie wanted nothing more than to spill her thoughts onto the pages of her journal. Scaling the ladder to her loft, Rylie froze at the top.

Someone had been through her stuff.

Her bed was torn apart. The drawers were pulled open and spilled across the floor. Her clothes were everywhere, and the package her mother sent was laid out as though someone had examined each item.

She hurried to pick it all up. Everything looked like it was intact, so the intruder hadn't found whatever they wanted. Rylie stroked Byron the Destructor's red nose with a frown. What did she have that someone would try to steal?

There was only one way to find out.

Rylie stalked out of the cabin. She found Amber chatting with another girl by the campfire, who fled as soon as she saw Rylie coming.

Amber covered her bandaged nose with a hand as if to protect it. "What do *you* want?"

"Why did you go through my stuff this time? Looking for something new to torture me with?"

"What?"

"Don't play dumb. I saw what you did! Why won't you just leave me alone?"

"I didn't do anything," Amber said. She looked genuinely confused. "God, you're such a *freak*." There wasn't much venom in her tone this time. She looked afraid Rylie would attack her again.

"Then who was it? Patricia? Kim?"

"We didn't do it, okay? Go away!" Amber hurried to follow the other girl out of camp, shooting a frightened look over her shoulder.

Rylie believed her. The intruder wasn't Amber. She was too scared to talk to her, much less invade her privacy again.

But if it wasn't them, then who?

Seven

Golden Lake

Waiting to see Seth again made the days drag. Rylie found herself watching the second hand creep around the face of the wall clock in the cafeteria when she should have been taking her turn wiping down tables or meeting with her group to go on a hike.

But evenings were the worst. She lay awake in bed most of the time, unable to sleep. Her mind spun with images of wolves and claw marks and full moons.

She wished she had some way of talking to Seth when he wasn't around. Rylie felt completely alone at camp. Nobody else knew what she was going through, or why she twitched every time something rustled in the bushes. She could hear and smell everything in the forest now. Her senses got sharper all the time.

Thursday came after eons of waiting. Rylie was so preoccupied with the idea of sneaking into the boys' camp that she couldn't make herself eat that night, and she ended up tossing her entire plate of vegetables into the trash.

After Louise turned out the cabin lights, Rylie snuck from her window and made her way down to the lake. She didn't need a flashlight. The night was bright and clear.

Picking her way down the rocks, she walked along the beach in search of Seth. The water lapped gently by her feet, which sank into the ground with every step.

"Seth?" Rylie called. The night was quiet enough that her voice carried farther than she expected, and she clapped a hand over her mouth as if she could take it back. Nobody responded.

She hugged her arms around herself as she waited. It smelled like fish this close to the water, but it wasn't an unpleasant odor.

Rylie took a deep breath. It painted a clear picture in her mind of deep, cold places and silvery fish flitting between swaying plants. It was hard to distinguish the different kinds of fish. She only knew the kinds that came in a can.

Something paler than the water splashed in the lake. Rylie stared as it approached and clearly became someone swimming.

Seth emerged from the water bare-chested and glistening. Rylie realized her jaw was hanging open, and she snapped it shut. He walked over and shook the water out of his hair.

"Aren't you cold?" Rylie asked in a tiny voice.

"It clears my head. Throw me the towel?"

She managed to look away from him long enough to find his towel folded neatly behind the rocks. Rylie was thankful the dark night hid her red cheeks, and she tried not to stare as he dried off and got dressed. "You didn't swim over, did you?"

He laughed as he sat to pull on his shoes. "No."

"How are we getting over there? It's kind of a long walk."

"I borrowed a canoe from the recreation shed," he said. "It's moored over there. Come on."

They rounded an outcropping of boulders. A small metal canoe was tied to one of the rocks, and Seth waded into the water to pull it halfway onshore. He held it while Rylie climbed in. The seat was damp and the metal was cold, but she kept her complaints to herself for once.

He pushed it out into the water before jumping in. Seth propelled them across the lake, the muscles in his arms flexing with every pull of the paddles.

"How do you feel now?" he asked.

"Stronger," she admitted. "More sensitive. I think I can smell better."

"You probably can. Your senses will never get to be as good in human form as are as an animal, but there's some bleed over. Are you getting more aggressive?"

Rylie frowned. "Aggressive? Why?"

"Another symptom."

"I don't know. Maybe. I'm not like that." *Not usually*, she added silently, but Rylie couldn't help but think back on her fight with Amber.

"Yeah? What are you like?" Seth asked. "What do you do when you're not rebelling at summer camp?"

Rylie trailed her fingers in the water. It was very cold, like any mountain lake at a high elevation. She couldn't imagine swimming in it during the day, much less at night. Seth wasn't even shivering. "I like art and movies. I go to a lot of museums. I write in my journal. What about you? What do you do when you're not hanging out with scary monsters?"

"I'm always hanging out with monsters," Seth said with a slanted smile.

"I'm serious, Seth."

He considered the question without breaking rhythm. Their canoe sluiced through the water and the other shore grew closer and closer. "I spend a lot of time with my family."

Something in his tone of voice made Rylie ask, "Do you like them?"

"Not always. But they're family, you know? You don't have to like them, but you need to love them." Seth changed the subject. "We're going to have to move fast when we get to camp. The counselors take turns walking around at night, and we can't be seen."

"Okay. Where are the books?"

Seth's sideways smile grew. "In one of the counselor cabins. It'll be a challenge."

"I'm up for it," she said with confidence she didn't feel. He lifted the paddles when they reached the shallows and drifted toward the shore. There was no sand on this side; the rocks jutted into the water and became a jagged cliff. Seth jumped out in the waist-deep water, guided their boat to a safe spot between the boulders, and lashed it into place.

"Can you climb?"

Rylie eyed the rocks. They looked at least thirty feet tall. "Maybe."

Seth hauled himself onto a rock and gave her a hand up. Grabbing what looked like a good handhold on the cliff, she was surprised to find she could lift her bodyweight effortlessly. Once she got going, he had to hurry to keep up with her.

"Not bad," Seth panted.

"Thanks," she said, looking down at the water. The cliff seemed even taller from the top.

The layout of Camp Golden Lake was just like its sister camp. The main office was near the shore, and they had to crouch behind a tree to avoid being spotted by a stocky counselor as he passed.

"Come on," Seth whispered as soon as the counselor's back faced them.

They crept along the wall of the office and hurried past the big fire pit. Seth led Rylie toward a squat log cabin behind the dining hall.

"Which one of the groups is yours?" Rylie asked, examining the trail directory nearby.

"Oh, that one." He waved vaguely in the direction of the water. "Quiet. Someone's coming."

Rylie got on her knees behind the sign, trying to make herself as small as possible. She felt like her pale blonde hair and white skin made her too visible in the darkness, unlike Seth, whose dark coloring didn't reflect the light as well.

The patrolling counselor passed. Rylie recognized his short yellow hair and wide shoulders: Jericho. His eyes swept over her hiding spot, and she tried to be invisible. Fortunately, his eyes didn't settle on them, and he moved on. She let out a heavy breath.

"How much further?" Rylie whispered.

"This is it," Seth said. "It's where the counselors hang out when they're not working."

"And they keep those books in here?"

He nodded. "The library is in the back room. Kids aren't allowed."

"No wonder, if they've got stuff on werewolves," Rylie muttered. "How do we get in?"

"The front door, of course."

She watched while he crouched in front of the door and inspected the lock. "You do have a way to get in, right?" she asked. He produced a leather wallet filled with rows of thin metal hooks. Her eyes widened. "Are those lock picks? You brought lock picks to camp?"

Seth flashed the Boy Scout salute at her. "Be prepared, right?"

He selected two of the picks and inserted them into the lock, his eyes falling half-closed as he concentrated on opening the door. Rylie shifted back and forth on her feet, alternating between watching him and the camp around them. Neither Jericho nor the other counselors were in sight, but she still had the awful feeling they were being watched.

Finally, he twisted both picks, and the lock clicked. Seth opened the door.

They went inside, shutting the door behind them. He turned on his flashlight. Harsh shadows crept up his cheekbones and forehead.

"That way," he said, pointing with the beam.

"The counselors are holding out on us," she observed as they navigated to a door at the back wall. There were vending machines with soda and chips—neither of which were offered to campers on her side—and even a big-screen TV in the corner.

There were no windows in the back room, so Rylie flipped on the light. A lone fluorescent bulb flickered to life.

Three of the walls were covered with tall cabinets, and a pair of free-standing cabinets occupied the middle of the room. Half the shelves had movies; the others had an array of worn books, many of which looked as old as the camp.

"Some library," she said. Seth stood on a stood to pull a dusty box from atop a cabinet. It was full of boring history books from the fifties and sixties. "How did you know to look for those here?"

"I didn't. I like to explore."

The most interesting book in the box wasn't a book at all, but a binder with a loose collection of hand-written pages. "Legends of Gray Mountain," Rylie read aloud off the cover.

"That's the best one. It was written by someone who said he used to hunt werewolves," Seth said. "Look here."

He took it from her long enough to flip to a section in the back. Rylie skimmed the page. "So there are five moons before the real transformation, counting the one where I got attacked. I only have three more before I become a..." She couldn't say "werewolf." It was too weird.

"Keep reading," he said. "That's not all."

The next page described what would happen on each of the six moons. The first was the bite. The second, which Rylie had just undergone, was mostly a mental change from human to wolf. The third involved some physical shift, which increased in the fourth and fifth moons, until the sixth... when she really became a monster.

Several hand-drawn illustrations showed what kind of physical changes she could expect: claws, teeth, fur. The works. It wasn't pretty.

She swallowed hard. "This does not sound good." Rylie flipped to the back, which had a short history of several different packs. Notes filled the margins, marking which werewolves had been killed by hunters. "So if I am becoming a—a werewolf... that means whoever attacked me is a person most of the time. Right?"

"Right," Seth said.

"Who is it?"

"It would make life a lot easier if I knew," he said grimly.

"I wish I could take this with me," Rylie said. "I want to read all of it. Is there a copy machine?"

"In the office."

"Let's do it. There's no way I can get everything I need out of this in one night."

"What do you expect to find?" Seth asked.

"I'm hoping for a cure. But why do they have all these books here? It doesn't make any sense," she said.

"It makes sense if this used to be an outpost before it became a summer camp. Silver Brook and Golden Lake have only been here for thirty years. Humans have been here much longer than that."

He peeked outside to make sure they were alone before hurrying across the path to the back door of the office. "Don't turn on the light," he warned as he picked the lock. "We don't want anyone to see us through the windows."

She nodded and went searching for the copy machine. It was gathering dust behind a tall stack of banker's boxes and a computer older than she was, but it hummed to life when Rylie pressed the power button.

Pulling all the pages out of the binder, Rylie arranged them into a neat stack and fed them through the paper tray. The copy machine thumped and whirred, flashing green light under the glass. She kept an eye on the windows and tried to block the light with her body.

Rylie barely breathed until the copying finished, certain that Jericho would storm in at any second. "Let's go," Seth said as soon as he grabbed the last of the pages.

They locked the office behind them and hurried back to the communal cabin. Rylie waited outside while Seth returned the original copy of The Legends of Gray Mountain to the cabinet.

"I want to get back to my side of camp," Rylie whispered, clutching the stack of papers to her chest. They stuck to the shadows as they jogged back toward the lake. "I don't feel safe here. I just know—"

"Hey! What are you two doing up?"

Jericho strode toward them. Rylie's heart sped. Seth took the papers and grabbed her hand.

"Run!"

They fled into the forest. Jericho crashed through the bushes behind them, tearing through the trees as though they were barely an obstacle. Her hand slipped out of Seth's. Too afraid to slow down, she increased her pace, darting deeper into the forest and further away from the trail.

She wove in and out of the trees. Rylie was fast. She was agile. She was running blind, and good at it. But her pursuer was better.

Someone blew through the forest behind her. Praying it was Seth, she pushed on.

Trees flashed past. The dirt thudded beneath her hiking boots.

It took too long to realize she was suddenly alone.

"Seth?" Rylie whispered, stopping short.

She was alone. What if Jericho had caught him? There was no doubt in her mind he wouldn't be as forgiving as Louise. Seth could get sent home, and then Rylie wouldn't have anyone to help her. The thought was frightening.

Tilting her face into the breeze, she took a short sniff, trying to detect Seth's odor. She felt stupid doing it, but she immediately found him. He wasn't far. She was confident she could follow the smell right to him.

There was another smell, too: musky, woodsy, and warm. It was a very strong odor, but it wasn't human. It wasn't exactly animal, either.

The werewolf. It was near.

Trembling, she took another long, slow sniff. It was on the move. The werewolf was coming toward her. Rylie watched the trees around her, trying to see what she knew had to be there.

It didn't come into her line of sight. It hung back.

Watching.

Did it recognize her? Did it remember attacking her almost a month ago? Or was it just trying to decide if she would be easy to take down?

"Come out," she called softly into the night. "You want to fight? Come get me."

The smell began to fade. It was leaving. Seth's smell was growing stronger, even though the breeze was blowing in the wrong direction now, and she could hear the crunch of his footsteps on pine needles.

She was torn between following the werewolf and reuniting with Seth. Rylie didn't need The Legends of Gray Mountain if she could get answers from the source, and her heart ached with the need to follow it.

She took too long to consider. All traces of the werewolf vanished.

Disappointed, Rylie went to Seth's scent. He was still wandering through the forest, and he looked surprised to see her. "You okay?" he asked.

Rylie nodded. She didn't want to tell him that she had tracked his scent. It was too weird. "Do you think he recognized us?"

"How would he know you?"

"Jericho caught me on this side of the lake the other day. He's—well, he's kind of terrifying."

"Hopefully he just thought you were a boy out of bed," Seth said.

"A boy with long blonde hair?"

"If it makes you feel better, I have good news. I kept a hold on this." He showed her the roll of pages copied out of The Legends of Gray Mountain.

"Great, I guess. Or not great. I don't know, Seth." Rylie sat on a felled log and cradled her head in her hands. "This is so much to take in. I didn't even believe in ghosts a month ago, much less werewolves. You know?"

He sat beside her on the log, slinging his arm over her shoulders in a comforting half hug. "Yeah. I do." Rylie's cheeks heated again.

"There's another full moon in a few days," she said. "What do I do?"

"I think you should lay low. The werewolf is a person, so it might come looking for you." She opened her mouth to speak, but Seth went on before she could. "I'm not trying to scare you. Just stay in big groups and don't get in trouble. I'll come help you out on the next moon."

"Am I dangerous until then?" she asked.

He gave her a serious look. "Maybe."

They made their way back to the lake. It was easy with Rylie's sense of smell. Seth took her to Camp Silver Brook in the canoe, but this time, their trip was silent. Rylie stared up at the waxing sliver of moon in the sky.

Why had Rylie, of all people, been bitten? She was going to become a wolf at the end of summer, and she hadn't done anything to deserve it.

She got out on the beach. Seth stayed in the canoe. "I'll see you on the full moon," he said, passing the papers to her. Their fingers brushed together. "Remember: lay low."

She climbed her way back to camp and looked for Seth once she reached the office. He waited in the boat, and although it was too dark to see his face, she could tell he was watching her go.

Rylie got into bed and huddled under the sheets. She didn't fall asleep.

It was a long time until morning.

Eight

Laying Low

For the next few days, Rylie followed Seth's orders and stayed in her cabin. She passed the time by reading The Legends of Gray Mountain by flashlight.

The young werewolf changes late at night when the moon is at its height. As he ages, he transform earlier and earlier, until finally, at full maturity, he can change when he chooses. In the early years, he is mindless, and he knows insatiable hunger.

Rylie stared at the words *insatiable hunger*. She shivered.

When she had to leave the cabin for activities, Rylie participated without arguing. She swam in the lake and went kayaking. She made bracelets, learned about edible flora, and took hikes. Amber still looked like she was afraid Rylie would explode, so they avoided each other. Louise was relieved.

"You've been doing great this week," she said when Rylie was helping clean up after a campfire dinner. "Thank you. I appreciate it."

She gave the counselor a weak smile. It was hard to rebel when all she could think about was becoming furry on the next full moon.

Rylie tried to get through all of The Legends of Gray Mountain, but she found herself returning again and again to the pages depicting what would happen every moon. The final werewolf looked like a normal wolf, but bigger and deadlier.

Her fear wasn't the worst part. No. The worst part was that she was almost excited.

She tried to banish the thought, just like she tried to ignore the meat on the buffet line, but it was hard without other distractions. Amber hadn't picked on her much since the archery incident, and everyone else was avoiding her, too. Making hemp lanyards was hardly more interesting than The Legends.

If nothing else, reading made her free time pass quickly. She started reading it by the campfire's flickering flames during her free time in the evening, too, brushing ash off the pages.

The next full moon. Rylie curled her fingers to examine them. She couldn't imagine claws bursting from the tips. It was ridiculous. Nightmarish.

But her symptoms were undeniable. One lunch, Rylie found herself hovering over the sandwich meat again, imagining the feel of it tearing between her teeth. They would have hamburger that night. She could smell it being ground in the kitchens even though they hadn't started cooking yet.

"I'm a vegetarian," she whispered to herself, like she had every day for the last couple of weeks. It sounded even feebler than before. Giving into eating red meat would *not* be laying low, especially after the scene she made over getting more vegetarian options.

Stubbornly selecting the tofu Louise had ordered and a bag of potato chips, Rylie took her lonely position at the end of a table. Nobody joined her, like usual. She didn't mind anymore. She was too preoccupied to talk.

A hulking man strode into the mess hall. His eyes scanned the room and briefly fell on Rylie.

Jericho.

She sank lower on her bench and tried not to look guilty, stuffing her food into her mouth faster than before. But Jericho didn't approach her table. Instead, he went to sit with Louise. If he told her that Rylie had been on the boy's side of the lake, then no amount of hiding would save her. She would be sent home.

Rylie tried to ignore the counselors as she finished her meal. As soon as she was done, she dumped her tray on the line and hurried outside.

"Rylie!" Cassidy ran to meet her. She was wearing a torn pair of jeans and a black shirt again, defying the summer heat. "Are you done with lunch already?

"Yeah," she said, glancing over her shoulder into the mess hall. Jericho and Louise were gone.

"You want to hang out?"

"Uh, no. Not right now, Cassidy," Rylie said. "Sorry, I have to get going."

"Why?" She stepped in front of Rylie's path to keep her from leaving. "I have some wicked new drawings to show you."

Jericho and Louise emerged from the back side of the building, strolling toward the offices. Ignoring her better instincts, which told her to go back to her cabin and avoid Jericho, she edged around Cassidy.

"Sorry. Maybe later."

The counselors paused to talk on the trail, and Rylie ducked behind a nearby tree to listen.

"Trouble on the other side, huh?" Louise asked cheerfully. "I always thought the boys were better behaved than any of the girls."

Jericho folded his arms and glowered. He was a shadow in the sunshine. "Maybe there was a girl being a bad influence on one of the boys."

"Did you see a girl over there?"

"I saw two kids, but it was dark. I couldn't identify them. Even so, I have reason to suspect one of them was a camper from your side of the lake."

"That's a problem," Louise said.

"Yes. Why would a girl cross over?"

She laughed. "Oh, probably the usual reasons. It seems like we catch a few couples in the act every year. Remember those two last year? Every single Tuesday night! It never amounted to any real trouble. They're just doing what teenagers do."

"It could become more trouble than we suspect," Jericho said. His voice was a low, dangerous purr. "Someone also broke into the counselor's cabin."

"Who do you think it was?" Louise asked. Rylie held her breath, peeking around the tree again. Jericho's back was to her. She couldn't make out his expression.

"I don't have enough evidence to make accusations. But if you find one of your girls *has* been getting out, I want to know about it."

Rylie grimaced. That sounded ominous.

"There are a couple problem campers this year, but I can't imagine them stealing anything," Louise said. "Are you sure it's that serious?"

"Oh yes."

She sighed. "All right. I'll let you know if I discover anything."

"Thank you, Louise," Jericho said.

They walked away. Rylie didn't follow—she had heard enough. Jericho knew she had been on the boy's side; he just didn't have enough "evidence." She didn't like to think how he was going to prove it, but she knew it was more important than ever to be on her best behavior.

At the beginning of the summer, Rylie would have chopped off her foot to be sent home. Now, over a month later, it was the last thing she wanted. The thought of changing into a werewolf at her dad's house made her sick. Going home wasn't an option. Not anymore.

There was a big campfire after dinner that weekend at the amphitheater. The fire pit in the middle of Silver Brook was filled with burning logs, and enough extra fuel was added to make the flames leap higher than the tallest benches. It was too hot to sit in the bottom row. Rylie took her seat in the shadows at the back to wait for announcements.

Cassidy sat beside her.

"How are you doing?" she asked, offering Rylie a chocolate bar from the s'mores ingredients stash by the fire.

Rylie reached out to take it, but her fingers were trembling violently. Instead, she sat on her hands. "Yeah. I'm fine."

"You sure? You've been acting weird," Cassidy said. "That's my job." She laughed, and Rylie figured she was supposed to laugh too. She mimicked the sound. It came out sounding forced and awkward.

"I guess I'm homesick," she lied.

"Getting any mail from your folks?"

"Sometimes." Rylie hadn't gotten anything since her mom sent her new clothing, but that was probably because they were too busy with divorce proceedings to write.

"I'm not." Cassidy unwrapped the chocolate bar and snapped a piece off in her mouth, chewing it on one side so her cheek bulged. "They hate me."

Rylie took a square of chocolate and let it dissolve on her tongue, watching the campfire. She couldn't think of anything nice to say to Cassidy about her family, so instead, she asked, "What about those drawings you wanted to show me before?"

Cassidy pushed up her sleeve to bare her wrist. The old ink was fading, but fresh line art ran from the inside of her elbow to the palm of her hand. A shaggy wolf bared his teeth as though chewing on the veins beneath the skin.

Rylie stared at it for too long. It almost looked alive. "That's a really good illustration," she said. Her voice was dead.

The director finally stepped in front of the fire to speak. Grateful for the distraction, Rylie pretended to be absorbed in the speech and ignored Cassidy. She didn't hear a single word.

Instead, she stared up at the sky.

The moon was almost full.

Nine

Teeth and Claws

Rylie woke up on the morning of the full moon with a note stuck to her loft window. Seth's sharp handwriting was on the outside: *Rylie.* Her heart sped a little. Seth had been there last night while she slept. The thought made her blush.

She pulled it from the window pane.

Meet me on the trail at the big pile of rocks after curfew. Eat a lot of protein at dinner tonight. You'll need your strength.

Rylie chewed her bottom lip as she considered his instructions. *After curfew.* It wouldn't be a problem, as far as the transformation went—The Legends of Gray Mountain indicated that the changes usually began around midnight in the early moons. But sneaking out of the cabin was getting riskier and riskier.

Of course, she couldn't change within the cabin, either. Rylie read the note one more time, then tucked it in the back of her journal.

On impulse, she tore a blank page out of the back and scribbled her own note. *I'll be there by ten.* She stuck it in the window. The note was missing by the time she returned from lunch.

She felt normal during the day. Normal enough that she almost doubted any of it was real. It would be easier to think it was all fantasy—werewolves weren't real, she couldn't become an animal, and there was no reason to fear the changing moods of the moon. But Rylie could deny her gold-flecked eyes or the near invisible scar on her chest no more than she could deny her suddenly overpowering sense of smell.

Rylie sleep-walked through her day in a haze, desperately wishing the sun wouldn't go down and the moon wouldn't rise. But they did. It grew darker and darker, and she grew more anxious.

At dinner that evening, Rylie recalled Seth's order to eat protein. Her stomach growled. She had a feeling she could eat pounds of tofu and it wouldn't be good enough. Not tonight.

The meatloaf smelled appealing, but her disgust overrode her cravings. Rylie had seen how cows were slaughtered, and the idea of eating them was sickening. She couldn't eat meatloaf. She just couldn't. Rylie scarfed down as much vegetarian food as she could and tried to ignore her hunger.

Louise visited her loft at bedtime.

"Are you okay?" she asked.

Rylie forced a smile. "I'm great. I'm having fun. I love camp."

The counselor gave her a knowing look. "If you're having a problem, I want to help you with it. Please. You know you can talk to me."

"Yeah, I know," she said with false enthusiasm.

Rylie waited a few minutes after Louise left, watching the sky outside. The full moon felt different than the new moon. Instead of feeling weak and sick, the beast inside was strong.

And hungry.

Even though she had eaten a huge helping of pasta, a big salad, and her usual tofu (which came in the form of fake turkey that night), her stomach growled as if she hadn't eaten in days. Rylie couldn't shake the thought of rare, dripping meat.

She changed from her pajamas into a pair of shorts and a loose tank top, hoping her partial transformation wouldn't lead to the clothes-ripping she always saw in werewolf movies. Slipping from her window feet-first, Rylie dropped to the ground outside and broke into a run.

Seth was waiting for her at the meeting place. He wore a white shirt that glowed in the night. Rylie was surprised. She had never seen him in anything but black before. "You ready?" he asked, and she nodded, unable to speak. "Come on."

They climbed deep into the trees, scaling the mountain until the path was no longer visible and they could look down on camp. There were only a few pinpoints of light. It looked peaceful from above.

"How are we going to do this?" Rylie asked.

"I've got a few things in my bag to keep you away from everyone," Seth said. "There's this one thing I got from a sporting goods store. It makes a smell like a wolf marking its territory. If I spray it around, it should keep your attention."

"So it's wolf pee," she said.

"I didn't say it was glamorous."

"Shouldn't we... I don't know... chain me to a rock or something? Aren't I going to be super strong?"

"Stronger than usual. Do you *want* to be tied up?" he asked.

Rylie glanced up at the moon. Part of her gave an emphatic, "Yes!" But a much larger part of her—a part that grew bigger by the second—bristled at the thought. "No, but if you're not going to chain me up, then how are you going to keep me out of camp? That marking stuff is only going to distract me."

He grinned. "I have a plan. Don't worry about it."

She barely heard him. She couldn't tear her eyes from the moon.

Shuddering, Rylie hugged her arms tight around her body and stepped into the shade of a tree. Tremors rippled through her bones. Her ribs and spine ached as though something was growing inside her.

"What's happening to me?" she whispered.

"The new and full moons are different," he said. "You change on the new moon because it makes the human weak, so the wolf emerges. On the full moon, the wolf becomes strong. It dominates you."

"Is that something else you read? Why haven't I seen it?"

"I can't bring you any more books. It's too risky."

"It can't be any riskier than hanging out with a werewolf," Rylie said. He knelt to open his backpack and pulled out a flashlight, something that looked like a can of hairspray, and a bundle of black straps. "What is that?"

"It's a muzzle," Seth said.

She understood: the werewolf curse was transmitted by biting. He had promised to stay with her for the night, but Seth wasn't going to risk the same fate she had.

He didn't trust her. The knowledge stung. "I don't want to wear it."

"It's only a precaution."

"I'm not an animal, Seth, no matter what happens to my body. I will not wear that thing."

"Rylie," he sighed.

"No."

"Are you going to be comfortable with your choice if you hurt someone?"

"That's why you're here," she said. "You have a plan."

"I'm going to do everything I can," Seth said, "but this is insurance."

Rylie shook her head. "I said no."

He hesitated, as though considering whether he could force her to wear the muzzle or not. Rylie glared at him until he put it back in the bag. "Okay. Are you ready to start changing?"

"Not really."

As though to point out she didn't have a choice, her body suddenly rocked with an internal blow. Dropping to her knees, Rylie braced her hands against the forest floor. Her head throbbed.

Ready or not, the change was about to happen.

She bent forward until she could rest her forehead on her fists. Her spine arched and her stomach heaved.

"It hurts," Rylie whimpered.

"I've got your back. I promise. I won't let you bite anybody."

Seth's voice was far away. The trees pressed in on her. The moon seemed to swell and grow larger as its silvery rays pounded through her skin.

Footsteps. He was leaving her.

"Seth!" she cried.

Blood spattered against the pine needles. Rylie stared down at the drops as they grew bigger. Her jaw hurt, and she reached up to touch her gums. Her fingers came away slicked with blood. Her canines lengthened and sharpened against her fingertips.

With a snap, the hinge of her jaw broke. Pain lanced down her spine and Rylie threw back her head. Tears sprung to her eyes as the bones around her nose crunched and expanded beneath the skin, spreading into a thousand tiny fissures. Her flesh wasn't elastic enough. It felt like it was tearing.

Rylie's mouth filled with blood. She tried to spit it out, but she had no more lips. They were stretched tight across her sharp fangs.

Her fingers raked the earth. From elbow to wrist, from knuckle to fingertip, her bones popped. The nails fell out. The claws that took their place were sharper than knives.

She was afraid. No. She was *horrified*. Rylie wanted to cry. There was no way she could deal with this—and definitely no way she was going to let Seth see her in such a state.

Unfortunately, Rylie was no longer in charge of her body.

Feet crunched against pine needles. Something was running from her. Running meant prey, which meant food.

The wolf was *starving*.

She shook the blood off herself and took a long stretch across the ground, feeling her joints pop and muscles relax. Pain wasn't important to the wolf, and she didn't care if her face felt like it had just been torn apart.

Sniffing the air, she detected a sour odor. Another wolf. She was in hostile territory. Pressing her nose to the bark of a tree, she breathed in every little bit of the odor. It smelled masculine and domineering, but the hormones were weak. Perhaps he could be challenged. Perhaps this could be *her* territory.

The smell was on another tree, and another. It led in the same direction as the pounding feet.

Some tiny part of her wanted to pursue on her hind legs—ridiculous. Dropping to all fours, she increased her pace to a trot, following the smell from tree to bush to rock.

Her prey sped up. She caught a glimpse of white between the trees, and she accelerated.

He ran, and she chased.

Rylie had become agile in the forest, but human intelligence interfered with the raw instinct that allowed her to utilize the natural paths in the wild. She was nothing compared to the wolf.

The prey was clunky and awkward, and he paused occasionally to spray pheromones on the trees. He was bright and easy to see in the dark, too.

He *wanted* to be chased.

It gave Rylie pause to realize Seth had deliberately made himself a target, but the wolf shoved her worries aside. Did it matter if the prey knew it was prey? It was prey nonetheless, and she was still hungry.

She angled to sweep around him, then leaped in front of his path.

He stopped. Changed direction.

The wolf jumped.

The prey absorbed the impact and rolled with her, planting his legs in her stomach to fling her over his head. She landed on her side.

Disoriented, she got up and shook herself.

He had taken the opportunity to run, and he was gone again. But she could still smell the fresh trail of pheromones.

She darted after him, and this time, she didn't bother taking it slow to conserve energy. Her stomach was a gnawing void beneath her ribs. Prey was close. Food was close.

The wind changed direction, and she stopped. The wolf could smell people on the air. They trafficked this land, and there were a thousand interesting odors—cotton, leather, denim, sweat, human foods and human perfumes. People were the best prey of all, and there were many of them just down the trail.

"Hey!"

A metal can clattered at her feet. The wolf lowered her head to sniff it—this was the source of the pheromone trail. Boring. It wasn't food.

She considered the human smells, and the camp below, and wondered how much human prey waited for her there.

"Hey! Hey, over here!"

Her head snapped around. The white-clad prey was higher on the mountain, waving his arms.

Baring her teeth, she ran, and he disappeared into the trees.

Something flashed in the corner of her eye. She smelled it an instant later: meaty, rich, and terrified. It was a deer separated from the herd. Helpless. Delicious. And much closer than the human.

She spun. Jumped on it.

It gave a scream as her claws sank into its hide. Her teeth tore into its flesh.

"Rylie, no! Stop it!" Meaningless sounds.

The deer thrashed. Its legs kicked out. One cloven hoof struck her face, and she circled around to another angle. The fawn tried to get back onto its feet, but before it could she leaped once more.

She bit, and bit again. The screaming stopped.

The original prey stepped into her line of sight. He didn't look as weak as he had smelled. He looked strong—maybe too strong for her to take tonight. Would he challenge her? Would he take her prize? Growling, she crouched over the deer to protect it.

"Oh, hell, Rylie," he said. "I'm sorry."

She ripped into the carcass, watching him out of the corner of her eye for any signs of attack. He only moved to step back into the trees. Good. She had her meal for the night. Throwing her head back, she loosed a long howl. *Her* territory. *Her* prey.

And then she began to feast.

The sun peeked over the edge of the mountains, spilling dawn across the tree tops. A sunbeam hit Rylie's eyes. She tried to cover her face, but something restricted her arms. Climbing to consciousness was a battle—she felt heavy and satiated, like she had been sleeping for weeks.

The first thing she saw when she managed to open her eyelids were her hands. Ropes circled her wrists and were connected to her ankles by another rope. Rylie shuddered. Her fingers felt like they were breaking, but it was painless this time. Her claws receded and fingernails grew in their place. It was over as quickly as it had begun.

Rylie was laying under something heavy—a jacket. It was warm, buttery leather, and it smelled like the tang of metal and burning coals. She hadn't realized it before, but that was Seth's distinct smell.

She looked up. His face hovered over hers.

It took Rylie a minute to remember how her mouth worked. It was difficult to assemble her thoughts into words, and translate that into the necessary motions to speak. "Seth," she finally said.

"Hey."

Realizing she was seated on the ground with her back against his chest, Rylie decided not to move. She was much more comfortable than she had been after the last moon. "What happened? Did we do okay?"

Seth untied the ropes around her wrists and ankles. "It doesn't matter. How do you feel?"

"I'm... good," she said. "Really good. I feel satisfied."

Seth's mouth drew into a hard line. "Good."

"Is my face normal?"

"You look fine, Rylie."

Her nose picked up the smell of drying blood. She sat up to look around and saw Seth's ruined white shirt a few feet away. Examining her hands once more, she found blood in the cracks of her palms and between her fingers. He must have used his shirt to wipe her off. "I didn't hurt you, did I?"

"No. Think you can stand up?" She was tempted to say no so she wouldn't have to move, but Rylie knew she had to return to camp. At her nod, Seth helped her get to her feet.

"Where did the blood come from?" she asked.

"Let's get you back to your cabin," Seth said. He was only wearing his undershirt now, but he didn't look bothered by the cool morning air.

"What about you? Won't you get in trouble?"

He almost smiled. "They can't send me home."

Rylie hugged Seth's jacket around her as they headed back to the trail. She wished she had worn pants instead of shorts. "I don't really remember what happened last night."

"It's better that way," Seth said.

He tried to shield her from something on the ground when they got to the side of the trail.

"What is that?" she asked, voice shaking. Seth didn't respond, so Rylie pushed him aside to see the body.

It was a fawn. She could tell because of the spots on its rump and the four spindly legs. The rest of it, however, was barely recognizable. Its throat was mangled, and its chest and stomach had been torn open, leaving the ribs jutting toward the sky like bloody spears.

She could almost remember it: the smell of fur, the taste of meat, the warmth in her belly as she ate. Rylie had killed a baby deer. It was the first meat she had eaten in years, and she had slaughtered it with her own teeth and claws. A single eye, forever unblinking, stared out of its bloody face.

Her knees gave out. Rylie drew her legs up to her chest and buried her face in her arms. She didn't hear Seth approach until he was crouching at her side. "It was an accident," he said. "I let you get away."

"I should have taken the muzzle," she whispered.

Seth touched her hand, and Rylie wrapped her fingers around his.

Ten

Co-Ed

Rylie started throwing up in the shower.

She cupped a hand over her mouth and ran for the toilets. Rylie could hear girls whispering in a tight cluster by the sinks as she heaved. Everyone was too afraid of her now to ask if she was okay.

She didn't want any help. Nobody could get rid of the guilt or the taste of deer in her throat.

When her stomach was finally empty, Rylie leaned her forehead against the cool porcelain and shut her eyes. The girls were still whispering. She didn't want to face them. She wanted to vanish.

A hand laid a damp towel across the back of her neck. "Rylie? Are you all right?" The voice was kind and familiar, but it took Rylie a minute to realize it was Louise.

She nodded without opening her eyes. She didn't feel any better. Rylie could see the fawn's staring eye and its bloody ribs. She needed to clear the memory from her mind, not the meat from her stomach.

Louise sat with her silently until everyone else finished in the showers. "I'm going to have someone take you to the infirmary," she said gently.

"I'm not sick," Rylie mumbled.

"Maybe, maybe not. You can just rest."

Unsurprisingly, Cassidy came to her side, offering her a hand to get off the floor. "Come on. Are you really sick, or are you just trying to get out of swimming this morning?"

Rylie made herself smile. "I've never liked swimming," she said. It was much easier than trying to explain why she had thrown up.

After the nurse took her temperature and administered anti-nausea medication, she laid face-down on the infirmary bed and pulled the blankets over her head. Seth had said she slept after eating last night, but she was still exhausted.

She sank into a deep sleep immediately. The fawn stared at her in her dreams.

Rylie wasn't sure when Louise came to bring her back to camp, but she felt more beaten after her nap than she had before taking it.

"Do you want to go horseback riding with the group?" Louise asked.

Remembering how the horses had reacted to her smell, Rylie shook her head. Louise didn't argue, so Rylie got the afternoon to herself in the cabin. She spent it poring over The Legends of Gray Mountain.

"There has to be a cure," she muttered. "There *has* to be."

Rylie read the sections on the curse again and again. They listed a half dozen ways to kill werewolves. She was, apparently, susceptible to silver bullets, aconite, fire, and decapitation. Considering three of those four things could kill anyone, and that Rylie didn't want to die, it didn't help. She didn't consider death a cure.

The only suggestion of an escape was a single sentence in the section describing the transformation.

If the cursed one changes on the sixth and final moon, he will change on every subsequent new and full moon until the end of his days.

If the cursed one changes?

Rylie wished she knew how to get a hold of Seth when he was on the other side of the lake. He knew so much more than she did.

She didn't sleep better that night, or the next night, or the next. And things got worse from there.

Louise had an announcement to make while they were roasting hot dogs over the fire that weekend. "How many of you like volleyball?" she asked. The campers responded with muttering and shrugs. Rylie didn't like volleyball—or any other sport, for that matter—and remained silent. "Great. I've signed us up to play tomorrow morning. I hope we're good at it, because there's going to be a little tournament against Golden Lake next Tuesday."

"Ooh, really?" purred Patricia. "Are the boys coming over here, or are we going over there?"

"They're coming over here."

Rylie perked up. "All the guys?"

"Any boy who signs up, but it's completely optional. Our own sign-up sheet for the tournament is on the mess hall door."

She stabbed thoughtfully at the coals of the fire with her poker, rolling over a hot dog someone had accidentally dropped amongst the coals. If Seth signed up for the tournament, it would be a perfect time to talk to him.

Rylie stood in front of the sign-up sheet during breakfast, studying the names listed. Amber and her crew had, of course, enrolled. Cassidy hadn't. Those weren't the kind of people she wanted to play with. But if signing up meant seeing Seth...

After staring at the sheet for several minutes—and making a line form behind her—Rylie finally signed her name on the bottom line.

They gathered at the volleyball court by the lake that morning.

"Two teams!" Louise called. "Kim is captain of the first team. Rylie, you can captain the second."

"I don't even know how to play volleyball," Rylie said.

"It's just to select team members. You don't have to do anything else." Louise gave her shoulder a gentle nudge. "Go on. Kim gets first pick."

Rylie and Kim separated out the group. Kim chose all of her friends—Amber, Patricia, and a few other shrews—and Rylie took whoever was left. Nobody looked thrilled to be on her team, and she didn't blame them. She was terrible at sports.

Louise tossed a volleyball to Rylie so she could serve. She held it aloft in her left hand, glaring at the ball like it had insulted her.

"Let's do this," she growled.

She threw the ball in the air and smacked it with her hand. It bounced over to the other side, and she jumped forward to knock it back when Patricia returned it. One of her teammates had to hurry out of Rylie's way when she lunged to hit it.

The ball struck the ground on the other side. One point.

"Your serve again," Louise said.

Rylie hit the ball harder this time. Patricia barely missed it. Another point.

Her pulse sped up. The last time Rylie played a game in gym, she had been clumsy and awkward and missed every shot. But now she was fast and accurate. The ball moved in slow motion.

Rylie bounced the ball over the net and leaped back to catch a spike. She knocked into a teammate with her shoulder.

"Watch it!" a girl yelped.

"Sorry," Rylie muttered. She was too distracted to care. She couldn't tear her eyes off the ball. Something about the speedy way it moved excited the wolf in her, like she was hunting again.

The other team threw the ball over, and someone on Rylie's side sent it back. Patricia struck it hard, and the volleyball rushed just over the net. Rylie dove forward, arms extended, and it bounced off her wrists. Amber struck it back to her side.

Rylie leaped up just in time. She spiked the ball and it hit the ground so hard it deflated.

"Yes!" she exclaimed. She grinned and raised her hand to high-five her teammates.

They all stared at her. It was like she had grown a tail.

Her hand slowly fell. They thought Riley was a freak for being good at volleyball, but they would have laughed at her if she had been bad, too. There was no winning. No matter what she did, they were going to hate her.

Her vision went red around the edges. The wolf was angry and Rylie was ashamed. The emotions warred inside of her, making her feel hot and sick.

"Don't worry about it, I've got another ball," Louise said. She tossed it over to Rylie's team.

Yolanda took the ball to serve, and Rylie sat on the bench to watch the game finish. She shouldn't have been surprised. Everyone was afraid of her, and a good game of volleyball wouldn't change that.

"Great job, Rylie," Louise said enthusiastically as Rylie shucked her knee pads into the basket after the game.

"Whatever," she mumbled.

"You're good. Did you sign up for the tournament?"

"Yeah."

"You're going to be a great asset to the team. Jericho will be excited."

Rylie's eyes snapped up to Louise's face. "Jericho?"

"He's helping me run the games. In fact, he'll be over for practice tomorrow with the boys who signed up," she said. "We'll have a skirmish before the real games start. Won't that be fun?"

I need advice, Seth, she wrote that night on a blank journal page. *Jericho is going to be in camp tomorrow. I'm afraid. I'm pretty sure he knows it was me at the boy's camp. What should I do?*

She stuck it in the windowsill and waited. Rylie tried not to fall asleep so she could see Seth take the note, but the hours passed too quietly. She dozed off sitting up against the wall.

When she awoke in the morning, the note was gone, and one from Seth took its place.

Don't worry. He has no proof.

Rylie crushed the note in her hand. Seth always seemed to visit when she wasn't around. She wanted to talk to him so desperately. Why didn't he ever wake her up? Was she afraid of her now that he saw her slaughter the fawn? Without Seth, Rylie would be completely alone.

Seth wasn't amongst the group of boys who signed up to play volleyball against the girls. They all warmed up after arriving the next day and began to play. Jericho stood on the sidelines with Louise. Rylie could feel him watching her.

The practice volleyball game was half-hearted. Most people hadn't seen anyone of the opposite gender since the beginning of summer, and more of the campers seemed inclined to flirt than play volleyball. The girls played against other girls while the boys played against other boys, but once they started playing each other, there was much more talking and laughing than actual volleyball.

After a few hours, the counselors stopped trying to keep everyone focused. They broke for lunch and the cooks brought boxes of food to them at the volleyball court. Rylie sat by the water to eat her sandwich, picking off salami and flinging it to the waiting birds.

"Louise was right. You're good at volleyball."

Rylie looked up. Jericho stood over her with his arms folded. He looked even more massive from the ground.

A sense of wolfish calm settled over her. She took a big bite out of her sandwich, chewing slowly while he stared at her. Rylie should have been afraid of him. She had been anxious about running into him for days. But now that she faced him, she felt nothing. What could he do to her? If she wanted to, she could rip his throat out.

When she finished her sandwich and he hadn't moved, she stood up and dusted sand off her shorts. "Do you want something?"

"You know what the punishment is for crossing sides of camp?" Jericho asked.

"Nope."

"On the first violation... nothing, really. You get some privileges taken away for a few days. Maybe confined to your bunk." He leaned in close to her ear. "But for a girl who's been fighting? For a girl who broke into the counselors' cabin? That's good enough to get sent home."

She took several large steps back to put distance between them. "Get away from me," she warned. The wolf was waking up. It would be too happy to take him on.

"I know it was you," Jericho hissed.

Rylie glared. "You can't prove anything."

"You weren't alone. Who did you talk into sharing your teenage delinquency?" he demanded. She bristled. "You look like you're getting mad. Do you want to fight with me?"

"No," she said. It was a complete lie. The wolf absolutely wanted to fight.

"Tell me who you worked with, and I won't have you sent home."

Rylie laughed. "Are you kidding me? If I did go sneaking over to that side of the lake—and I'm not saying I did—then telling you who I was with would only mean both of us would get expelled."

"You're trouble, Rylie Gresham. Aren't you?"

"Of course not," she said. "I'm an innocent little angel."

Jericho stabbed a finger at her. "You better believe I'm watching you. Step one foot out of line again—"

"Yeah. Big words."

Rylie crumpled her sandwich wrapper and flicked it at his chest. She returned to the group, trying to suppress a grin while Jericho fumed on the beach. Before getting bitten, she never would have had the courage to be so blatantly anti-authority.

Maybe becoming a werewolf wasn't *that* bad.

For the next few days, Camp Silver Brook buzzed over the volleyball tournament. The girls playing on the team were even excused from regular activities to practice. "It's supposed to be a casual, friendly rivalry, but I'm a little competitive," Louise confided in Rylie after one practice session.

The night before the tournament, they held a big cookout at the main campfire. Rylie sat down with Cassidy.

"You going to watch the game with me tomorrow?" Cassidy asked. "Sounds stupid and boring. Might as well talk through it, right?"

"I can't. I'm on one of the teams," Rylie said.

Her upper lip curled. "I didn't peg you for a team player."

Rylie snorted. "Trust me. I'm not."

Louise came over. Her face was grim and unreadable, and her hands were squeezed together. "Can I talk to you, Rylie?"

"Sure. What is it?"

"Somewhere private," Louise said.

The counselor led Rylie a short distance away, far enough that nobody could hear them talking. The sun dropped below the trees, casting the forest in golden twilight. "What's the problem?" Rylie asked.

"I'm so sorry," she said, taking Rylie by the shoulders. A muscle in her cheek spasmed. "I know you were looking forward to the volleyball tournament. Wait. No, that's stupid." She took a deep breath. "Okay. I spoke to the administrators in the office. Your mother is coming to pick you up in the morning."

Rylie felt dizzy. She was getting sent home? The new moon was in a week, and she couldn't do it without Seth. "Were you talking to Jericho? Don't listen to him," she pleaded. "He's crazy. He's out to get me. You can't send me home! Please!"

"It's not that," Louise said, her face drawn tight.

"Then *what*? Why am I going home?"

"Rylie... it's your dad."

Eleven

The City

Rylie left a note for Seth wedged in the window. *My dad had a heart attack. I have to go to his funeral. I'll be back before the new moon.* The ink was smudged on the last sentence where she tried to blot away her tear drops.

Her mom, Jessica, showed up at ten thirty the next morning. Rylie watched the camp disappear in the side mirror, a feeling of dread weighing on her shoulders.

"How has it been at camp? You haven't written," Jessica said when they hit the highway.

"It's fine."

There was a reason Rylie hadn't written to her mom. Her dad was more than family; he was a friend. She could talk to her dad. But Rylie hadn't had a conversation with her mom that hadn't ended in a fight since middle school.

The drive back to the city was long. Forest and mountains turned into rolling hills. Hills turned into suburbs and small towns. The small towns became big, and then they were at the city, with all its narrow streets and mirrored skyscrapers.

Rylie felt claustrophobic, and stepping into her mom's high-rise condominium only made it worse. She stood in the doorway to her room with a bag over her shoulders, staring around at the posters she had put up to make her mom's place feel less lonely. Classic movies, concert posters, art prints. They looked stupid now. Meaningless.

The walls in the condo were a blue-gray color that felt alien and unnatural after the warm tones of the wild. Rylie wiggled her toes on the cold ceramic tile flooring and imagined it was dirt.

She sat on the end of her bed. Jessica had picked out an array of white pillows and a white comforter for it, and everything was just as tidy as when she left. A few of her books from home were on the shelves. Her backpack for school was on the floor of the closet. She even had clothes in the dresser. The only new thing was a white vanity that was not, and never had been, to Rylie's taste.

Her reflection in the mirror had red-rimmed eyes and puffy lips. She had been crying for a long time.

Rylie found her spare charger and plugged in her cell phone. The light came on immediately, but the battery was completely depleted, so it wouldn't turn on until it charged.

She stared out the window at the narrow black strip of street. A jogger passed on the sidewalk, white tennis shoes flashing beneath him. A woman pulled a dog away from a toppled trash can. A pair of children played jump rope.

Something ached inside of her. Rylie knew she should have been sad, but she felt too numb to feel anything now.

Her dad would never jog again, or walk a dog, or play jump rope. Just like that, he was gone.

Jessica brought her a black dress and shoes. "I know you don't have anything for... you know," she said, laying them across Rylie's mattress. "I hope you like this dress. Your aunt helped me pick it out."

"Is he really dead?" Rylie asked.

"Oh, honey." Jessica reached out like she was going to hug Rylie, but she stepped out of the way before her mom could touch her.

"I just need to hear it from you. I need to know it's real."

Her mom covered her mouth with a trembling hand, and tears rolled down her cheeks. She shook her head once and walked out of the room, shutting the door behind her. Rylie stared after her. It felt like a giant hole had been carved out of her chest.

She tried on her dress in front of the full-length mirror. It was modest, like everything her mom bought. The hem hit at the knee and the sleeves were short. The scoop neck was just wide enough to show off her silvery claw scars. Rylie wondered, distantly, what Seth would think of the dress.

It felt like a long time since she had really looked at herself. Her reflection had changed over the course of three moons. Her fine blonde hair reached her elbows now, as though the transformations made it grow faster. Her gangly, knobby arms and legs had fleshed out with muscle. Her skin had a healthy copper tan.

Strangest of all, the gold veins in her eyes were spreading. She looked more and more like the wolf as time went on, and less like Rylie.

She kind of liked it. She looked strong and healthy. Like she could take anything on.

Even her dad's funeral.

Her phone chimed and buzzed. Rylie turned it on to find twelve new text messages and several missed calls. They were all from the guys she hung out with at school. She hadn't told anyone she was being sent to camp for the summer, so they had been trying to meet up with her for weeks.

The most recent one was from her friend Tyler. Rylie called him back.

"Hey, what's up?" she asked.

"Rylie? Wow! I thought you were dead!"

She rolled her eyes. "You're not too far off. I saw your text message."

"Yeah! You want to see Black Death at The South Den tonight? You're the only one I know who likes them but me."

"The South Den is in a really bad part of town," Rylie said.

"Yeah, but it's Black Death unplugged! They only sent out a hundred invitations to this thing. I got passes because my cousin's a barista there. Come on, Rylie. You can't miss it."

She bit her lower lip, staring at her reflection across the room. Rylie looked grave and dark in the mirror. She didn't think it was a good idea to go out and have fun when she was only in town for her father's funeral.

But what else could she do? Sit at home with her mom?

"Sure," Rylie said. "I'll be there."

Jessica knew better than to ask Rylie where she was going. She wore a loose skirt and her favorite pair of Converse so she could walk to the train station. The three blocks to the station had seemed like a long distance last time she visited, but after weeks of hiking, Rylie found herself passing the stop instead of boarding the train. The South Den was only a few miles away. She felt restless and wanted to move.

The art district became darker and dirtier as she moved south. Shops had bars over their windows and half of the street lamps didn't work. Rylie ignored the people begging for money and walked on.

The South Den was a coffee shop in an alley behind a condemned bank. They rented out the old money vault, and the only way inside was to take a road underneath the building and pass through metal doors. Rylie had to wait outside for Tyler, since she didn't have passes, and the bouncer watched her with one eye while he screened other entrants.

Black Death was too popular for such a small venue. The street was packed with fans hoping to catch a glimpse of them, pressing to get closer to the door.

She spotted her friend above the crowd and waved her arms over her head.

Tyler bounded toward her with a wide grin, impervious to the press of the crowd. His front teeth were separated by a big gap and his hands were too big for his body. "Rylie! How's it hanging?"

"Good," she said cautiously, bracing herself for the questions: Why were her eyes a different color? How had her hair grown so long? And why did she look so weird?

But Tyler gave her one of his tickets without batting an eye. "Let's get in, huh? It's cold out here!"

Of course he didn't notice. Tyler never noticed anything. She almost laughed with the relief of not having to deal with her problem for once.

The South Den was already packed in anticipation of the show. Roadies assembled the drums on stage. The limited number of tickets meant it wasn't as crowded as usual, so Rylie easily found an empty table in a dark corner. She wrinkled her nose at the stench of body odor and cigarette smoke.

Tyler jumped on the bar stool across from her. "How's your summer going?" she asked.

"It's been wild. You'll never guess what happened. Remember Teri?"

It took her a few seconds to bring a face to mind. "You mean Teri Haynes? That girl you stalked since spring break hoping she would notice you?"

Tyler's grin widened. "She finally noticed me."

"No way."

"We've been dating for two weeks. She's my girlfriend now! Nuts, huh?"

Her smile grew fixed. "Yeah. Nuts. Teri and Tyler. That's... cute."

Tyler checked his phone. "I'm going to meet Teri outside. I'll be right back. With my *girlfriend*." Rylie gave a weak laugh and watched him go.

Girlfriend: the dirtiest of dirty words. Girlfriends interfered with friend-time and turned her guy friends stupid. Rylie hated it every time one of the boys she hung out with got a new girl because it meant their fun was over until the relationship ended.

No matter how much she liked the band, Rylie never would have come if she knew it meant tolerating a *girlfriend*.

He returned with Teri in tow.

"Hi!" she sang in a too-bright voice. "I'm Teri!"

"I know," Rylie said dully. "We had chemistry together."

"Oh yeah! Are you taking AP chem next year?"

She stared at Teri. Rylie didn't want to make friendly conversation. She had seen Tyler date a half dozen girls, and none of them had lasted long. Teri wilted under her gaze.

"I'm going to get coffee," Tyler said, oblivious (as always) to the change in mood.

"I'll come with," Teri said, shooting a cold look at Rylie.

Rylie didn't understand why most other girls didn't like her. She suspected her blonde hair and skinny physique was a contributing factor. A lot of her friends' past girlfriends had hated her for it.

The singer took the microphone and the band started to play. She barely listened. Rylie didn't want to be at The South Den with Tyler and Teri, or anybody else, for that matter. She wished she could be with Seth instead. It scared her to think of him alone at camp with the werewolf. She wondered if Seth had friends that hated his girlfriends, too.

Tyler returned balancing several cups of coffee in his arms. He set one in front of Rylie and took a seat. Teri draped herself over him like a hungry octopus, and it was all Rylie could do to keep from rolling her eyes.

"It's a mocha cappuccino," he said. "Your favorite, right?"

She took a long drink. Her sense of taste had improved with her smell and she could make out all the subtle flavors of the coffee bean. They had roasted it an hour ago at most. Rylie let out a happy sigh. "This is amazing. I haven't had any coffee all summer at camp."

"You've been at camp, huh? Is it over already?" Tyler asked. She shook her head. "What are you doing back?"

"My dad died."

His eyes widened. Teri's hands flew over her mouth. "I'm so sorry!" she cried. "Are you okay? Maybe you should—"

She cut Teri off. "I'm fine." Tyler looked incredulous, so Rylie repeated, "I'm *fine*. Don't worry about it." She wasn't lying, not exactly. "Fine" may not have been the right word for how she felt, but Rylie didn't know how else to describe the emptiness between her ribs.

Teri finished off the last half of her drink in one gulp. "Let's get more," she said, giving Tyler a significant look.

Mentioning dead family members was the perfect way to kill the mood for the rest of the night. Rylie tried to bring up some of her favorite movies that Tyler also enjoyed, but he was too distracted by Teri's attempts to suck his face off to converse.

She tried to enjoy the music instead. Rylie liked Black Death, and they were even better performing a small venue. But she just couldn't get comfortable. The walls of the coffee shop were too close. The ceiling was too low. The music was too loud. Why had Rylie gone to such a place?

Rylie gave up after three more songs. The wolf couldn't stand it anymore.

"You know what? I'm going for a walk," Rylie said, interrupting Teri and Tyler in the middle of their make-out session.

"I'm bored here. We'll come too," he said, grabbing Teri's hand and pulling her along.

Rylie knew he wasn't bored. He was worried about her. Tyler had always been way too sympathetic.

The crowd mobbed them as they left. Hands grabbed for their jackets and tickets, hoping to get into their empty spots. The bouncer pushed everyone back long enough so Rylie could squeeze through, and she ducked further down the underground street.

"Aren't we going up to the surface?" Teri asked, clinging to Tyler's arm.

"I thought I'd walk to the subway station from here," Rylie said. The road underneath the bank building ran a few blocks and emerged right next to the train.

"I don't think it's safe."

"It'll be fine!" Tyler said. "You can just hold me if you're scared, babe." He winked at Rylie and pulled Teri closer with his arm around her waist.

"Tyler, please," Teri complained.

Rylie groaned. This was even worse than sitting at home with Jessica.

Tyler and Teri followed her down the tunnel. It was marked by yellow lights near the roof every few yards, leaving large swaths of the road in darkness. Their footsteps echoed against the concrete walls. The further they got from The South Den, the louder every little movement became.

"Are you sure you're okay?" Tyler muttered to Rylie when Teri released him for a moment to stare anxiously around the tunnel.

Rylie responded by staring at him. What was she supposed to say? He didn't look at her longer than a half second at a time, and she wondered if he had finally noticed her eyes.

"I don't want to scare you guys, but I think we're being followed," Teri whispered. Rylie glanced over her shoulder. Three formless men in bulky jackets were down near the curve in the tunnel. Their hoods were pulled over their heads. They could have been anyone.

When Rylie sped up, their followers sped up too. There was no mistaking their intentions. The men were trying to catch up like the werewolf had on the night she was attacked. Rylie, Teri, and Tyler were being hunted.

"They must have come from The South Den," Rylie said. She surprised herself with how detached she sounded.

"They probably want to buy our tickets to the Black Death gig," Tyler said.

Everyone knew that wasn't true, but nobody had to say it. The word *muggers* hung unspoken in the air around them. Teri clung harder to Tyler's arm.

They ducked down a side tunnel. It wouldn't take them to the train station, but Rylie thought it might get them to the surface faster. The men rounded the turn not long after they did, speeding their pace.

The thrill of the hunt ran through Rylie, and she had to close her eyes to keep from falling over. She was suddenly so hungry.

"There's a police station three blocks down," Tyler whispered. "If we hurry..." Hurry? Ridiculous. Rylie wasn't going to run. She wasn't prey.

"You're following us!" she called, turning to face them. "Why? What do you want?"

"Stop it," hissed Tyler. Teri clung to his arm. "What are you doing? Are you trying to get us killed?"

Rylie saw a flash of silver and smelled the tang of gunpowder. One of them was armed. His words smelled like ammonia to her sensitive nose. "Give us your wallets and jewelry. Everything."

The wolf grew still within her.

"Oh my God, oh my God," Teri whimpered, starting to empty her pockets. Rylie didn't move.

"Did you hear me? Money! Jewelry! Now!" he snapped. His friends flanked him. She didn't smell any other weapons, so she knew they were only meant to be intimidating. The three had one firearm between them.

"Rylie," Tyler said urgently while he set his cell phone on the ground.

The man with the gun moved forward to pick up what Teri and Tyler had dropped. The gun wavered.

"You too, blondie," rasped the man on the right. He was trembling. The wolf smelled sickness on them, the kind of weakness and disease that came from drug abuse.

Rylie flared her nostrils and sniffed. The gun had been fired recently, but she didn't smell fresh gunpowder. It wasn't loaded. They were being mugged by a gun without bullets. Her lips pulled back to bare her teeth in what must have looked like an uncomfortable smile.

He shoved the gun against her forehead. "You want to die, kid?"

Teri wailed.

Rylie's hand lashed out and her fingers raked down his gun arm. He shouted, dropping the gun.

Everyone was too shocked by her reaction to move. Rylie rammed her shoulder into his gut, shoving the mugger against the wall, and his head cracked against the concrete.

She jerked him back and flung him to the ground. The wolf pounced, pinning him beneath her knees. "Hungry," Rylie murmured, and his eyes went wide.

Her fingers tightened on his throat. Meat. Fresh and hot. She could already imagine it spilling across the asphalt and steaming in the cool night air. She could imagine the tang of blood, the satisfying tear between her teeth.

Like the fawn.

She wavered above him, lip sliding down over her teeth.

"You're crazy, bitch!" one of the other men shrieked. Their feet pounded as they fled.

The wolf registered the odor of feces—the man she pounced had soiled himself—but Rylie wasn't listening to it anymore. What had she done? She attacked a man with a gun. She could have been shot.

He shoved her, and Rylie didn't fight back. She sat down hard on the asphalt. The mugger scrambled to his feet and fled in the same direction as his friends.

"Are you guys okay?" Rylie asked, but Teri was pulling on Tyler's arm.

"Let's get out of here!" Teri urged.

Rylie turned to Tyler, hoping to find some kind of sympathy or gratefulness, but he looked just as pale and terrified as his new girlfriend. "What's wrong? I saved you two from those guys. Why are you—?"

"Jesus Christ, what is wrong with you?" Tyler asked.

"She's a freak! Tyler, please—hurry!" There it was again: freak. The word made Rylie's hair stand on end.

They ran too, leaving her alone in the tunnel. She drew her knees to her chest and hugged them, burying her face against her legs.

Her shoulders began shaking, and before Rylie could stop herself, tears poured down her cheeks. Her entire body shuddered. All the stress and pressure of the summer flooded out of her at once. "Oh God," she whispered into her arms.

Rylie was truly alone.

The grief struck her a moment later. She had been trying to block it out ever since Louise told her what happened to her dad, but it finally crashed into her.

He was dead. Rylie's dad was really dead.

She wept. Her cries echoed down the tunnel and bounced back to her magnified a thousand times over, like the howl of wind through trees on the peak of the mountain.

Rylie sat in the tunnel until her tears turned into dry sobs and then into silent trembling.

There was nothing left in her an hour later.

Rylie took the train home, leaving Teri and Tyler's valuables in the tunnel. Jessica was still awake when she entered the condo.

"Did you have fun?" she asked when Rylie passed her.

"Yes," Rylie lied.

She locked the door to her bedroom and didn't come out for a long time.

The funeral service wasn't for three more days.

Earlier in the summer, Rylie would have leaped at the chance to come back to the city. She had missed the art galleries, the theaters, and the parks. Now she didn't even want to leave her room.

Rylie hated to admit it, but she missed Gray Mountain. The big city park wasn't the same. The trees were too far apart. The bushes were too manicured. The brook really was a brook instead of a broad river. It babbled over smooth, colorful rocks instead of roaring over cliffs and crashing into boulders.

The wolf in her didn't think much of the park, either. Rylie couldn't keep herself from growling at a pigeon when it landed near her. A mother with a stroller hurried past, shooting her looks out of the corner of her eye.

Freak. She could almost hear Teri spitting the word at her.

Her room was like a cage, but it was better than the city.

Rylie avoided Jessica until the morning of the service. They had to ride to the cemetery together. They met at the car, and Jessica gave her a brief appraisal before getting in. "You look good," she said.

"Thanks," Rylie said, staring pointedly out the window.

"Has something changed? Are you wearing contacts now?"

"No."

Her mom dropped the subject, and they went to the cemetery in silence.

The day was too sunny and windy to be properly mournful. Rylie stood by the grave while the pastor read his eulogy. He said that Rylie's dad had been a wonderful influence in the community, and a loving family man, and something about ashes and dust and God. Rylie wondered what kind of terrible God would curse her and kill her dad in the same summer.

There weren't many people at the service: Rylie and Jessica, Uncle Jack and his family, and a handful of employees. Rylie's dad always had a big heart, but few friends.

She dropped a flower on his coffin as they lowered it into the ground. "Miss you," she whispered. The wind rose a little higher and tore the scarf from her neck, sending it dancing through the air across the graveyard. Rylie didn't bother chasing it.

"I'm so sorry for your loss," said his executive assistant, Tracy, at the church after the service.

"Thanks," Rylie said.

"I'm sorry for your loss," mumbled another employee as he passed.

She wanted to crawl under the carpet and disappear. How many people were sorry for her loss? And how many of them really cared?

Everyone left the church. Rylie and her mom sat in one of the back pews. She toyed with a cracker off one of the platters the church bought for the reception. Rylie snapped off a corner and let the crumbs hit the church's floor.

"He left you everything," Jessica murmured. She dabbed at her eyes with the same tissue she had used for the last half hour. "At the final divorce hearing, he told me that he revised his will. Everything's yours. His house. His belongings. His investments. Even his business, if you want it. It's all going to be held until you turn eighteen."

Jessica's fist tightened on the tissue. The fact that Rylie's dad had won the family business in the divorce—and then gone on to will it to his daughter, rather than the ex-wife who used to run it—must have stung.

"Who's going to manage it until then?" she asked.

"Richard. He was in charge while your father and I went through the divorce anyway. Tracy can help him with whatever he doesn't know," Jessica said.

"Great."

Even though Rylie's mother had all but told her she was now very rich, she didn't feel excited. How could she, when the price was so high?

"You don't have to return to camp. I know you never wanted to go. I'm sorry we made you... made you leave. It was wrong." Jessica tried to sound upbeat. "You can stay with me in my condo. There's a great high school in the neighborhood."

"No." Rylie gazed at the cross at the front of the church. "I want to go back as soon as possible. Tomorrow."

"Tomorrow? Are you sure?"

"Yes."

Her mom left her in the church. There was nothing more to say. Rylie didn't want to live in Jessica's condo, and she didn't want to meet any of her boyfriends.

She sat alone for a long time. Rylie hadn't cried at the funeral, but her eyes began to sting. Two wet circles plopped on the Bible in front of her. Once she started to cry, it was hard to stop.

Sniffling and wiping her eyes on the back of her wrist, Rylie knelt at the prayer stool by the altar. She had brought her old rosary from communion, and wrapped it around her hands before clasping them together. She stared at the pulpit and gathered her thoughts.

Rylie wondered what she could say and what pleas she could make. If there was one question she needed to have answered, what would it be?

"Why me?" she finally whispered to the cross.

Nobody responded.

Twelve

The Fourth Moon

Jessica didn't linger when she dropped off Rylie.

"I'll see you in August," she said without looking at her. It was the only time they spoke on the entire ride over. Rylie took her bag out of the back seat and gave a small wave before hiking back to Camp Silver Brook.

She felt strange walking the path between the highway and the camp. It seemed like a lifetime since she had taken the trail with her dad wheezing at her side. Rylie was embarrassed to think that she had found him so humiliating in front of the other campers. Why had she cared what they thought anyway? She should have hugged him before he left. She should have...

Taking several slow, deep breaths to clear her thoughts, Rylie kept hiking. The further she got into the forest, the more relaxed she felt, and the more distant the city and her father's funeral became. Amber and her gang couldn't see her crying. Even if she had scared them off, there was nothing like a good breakdown to make her a fresh target again.

She found Group B's campsite empty. The schedule on the door of Louise's cabin showed that they were at a first aid class for the morning, and having a picnic later. Perfect. She could unpack before having to deal with anyone.

Byron the Destructor took his usual place on her bedside table where he could watch her sleep. Her shorts and pants went in the bottom drawer of the tiny dresser, and her shirts and sweaters went in the top. The journal stayed safely in her back pocket.

Rylie sat on the edge of her cot, surveying the loft and the beds below. She still didn't care for her roommates, but being back on the mountain where the air was fresh and the sun was bright was more calming than she expected. The city and felt messy and brain-shatteringly cacophonous. Here, everything was right.

Louise found Rylie writing in her journal on the cabin steps after the first aid class ended. She took a seat beside her.

"When did you get back?" Louise asked.

Rylie didn't look up. "Not long ago."

The counselor waited in silence while the nib of Rylie's pen scratched against the page. Louise turned her whistle over and over in her hands as though trying to decide what to say.

"If you want to talk, Rylie, I'm here. You're having a hell of a summer. I can't do anything about it. I probably can't even understand what you're going through. But I can listen."

"Thanks Louise," she said, and for once, she meant it. Rylie couldn't describe the werewolf problem without sounding crazy, but knowing she had someone on her side other than Seth, was who was elusive at best, comforted her.

She napped fitfully in her cabin that afternoon. Rylie dreamed of chasing a fawn in the forest, watching its spotted back bounce between the trees. It wasn't fast enough to escape her. She sank her teeth into its throat, and by the time it hit the ground, the fawn had become her father. His empty eyes stared at the sky.

Rylie screamed and screamed, but nothing could bring him back—she had killed him, he was gone, and she could still taste his blood on her tongue.

Her pillow was damp with tears by the time she awoke. The other girls chatted below her, painting their toenails as they waited for dinner. She smothered the sounds of her sobs underneath a blanket and stuffed a fist in her mouth so they wouldn't hear.

When they left, Rylie took a clean page out of her journal and prepared to write a note to Seth. Her fingers were shaking. *I'm back, Seth,* she began, but his name was barely legible. A tear rolled off her chin and blotted the ink.

Rylie flung her pen against the wall.

"Damn it!" she yelled, balling her fists in her hair.

Something moved in the trees beyond her window. She slid closer so she could see, scrubbing her cheeks dry with her hands.

Seth.

He lurked in the shadows, too distant to make out his expression. Rylie didn't need to see it to know he was looking back at her.

She pulled her boots on and dropped out the window. He greeted her by walking into the trees, and she followed silently. They stopped once the cabins were out of sight, and Seth gave her his slanted smile. "Hey," he said.

Rylie tried to smile back. It didn't work. Her chin trembled, and she dropped her head so he couldn't see the tears welling in her eyes.

His arms wrapped around her, and she rested her cheek against his chest. Seth's smell was comforting. She had missed him back in the city. Any thoughts of demanding answers from him fled her mind as she leaned into his embrace, and his hand smoothed small circles over her spine.

"I was so embarrassed the last time I saw him," Rylie whispered. She didn't need to tell him she was talking about her dad. "I wanted him to go away. I was so angry. I didn't... I should have... I mean, I thought I hated him."

"He knew you loved him," Seth murmured against the top of her head.

"But I should have told him. Why did he have to die?" She rasped the words so softly that she wasn't sure Seth would be able to hear her.

"Rylie..." He let out a long sigh. "Dying is as natural as being born, and all of us have to face it someday. Some sooner than others. It's difficult to understand the meaning of it all. The question isn't, 'Why do we die?' The correct question is, 'Why do we live?'" Seth's hand stilled on her back. "My father died when I was very young."

She looked up at him. His gaze was distant. "I'm sorry."

"Why did he live?" Seth mused. Rylie knew he wasn't asking her, so she didn't respond. "My father was the best in his field. Very accomplished. But my mother told me once that my brother and I were his greatest pride, and that we gave his life meaning. He lived for us." He finally looked down at her, and his brown eyes were warm. "I am sure your father felt the same about you."

Seth's face was so close to hers. At any other time, Rylie's heart would have been racing, but the weight of sadness pulled her down.

"He was my best friend," Rylie said. Her chest hitched. "I think he knew that."

"I'm sure he did."

She wrapped her arms around him. "Thank you, Seth." He held her for another minute. By the time he stepped back, her eyes had dried.

"The new moon is coming soon," Seth said.

Rylie was grateful for the change in subject. It was easier to deal with the mind-bending horror of being a monster than her dad's death. "I get it if you don't want to help me again," she began, but he interrupted her.

"We can do better this time. Last time almost worked, but I didn't expect the distraction. We could try bear bells to keep your attention on me."

"No," she said. "It was crazy to make yourself a target for a half-changed werewolf. Crazy and stupid and dangerous. What if I'd mauled you instead of the fawn?"

"I'm not that easy to maul."

"I won't let you put yourself at risk." Rylie worried her bottom lip between her teeth, choosing her next words carefully. "I thought about how we should do it this time, and I decided I want to be tied up."

"It's the new moon. You won't be as aggressive as you were on the full moon," Seth said. "I can control you. I'm sure of it."

"You were sure last time, too. It's not your fault I killed the deer, but I'm not willing to do it again. Okay? Just try to find somewhere safe. I don't want to hurt anything." Rylie silently plead with her eyes.

"It's your choice."

"Thank you." Rylie frowned. "You would tell me if there's a cure, right?"

His expression became blank. "What do you mean?"

"The Legends of Gray Mountain made it sound like there might be a way to avoid turning into a werewolf. Do you know anything about that?"

"You can't be immunized against a curse," Seth said.

"I know that."

"I promise I will tell you if there's a cure," he said. "It's time for me to go, but I'll see you on the new moon." The side of his mouth curled up in a smile. "Are you going to eat meat at dinner like I told you this time?"

Rylie winced. "I don't know if I can do it. I threw up after the deer incident."

"Better steak than a fawn, right?"

He had a point.

The night of the new moon, Rylie spent a good twenty minutes at the buffet line. They had all the ingredients for hamburgers: buns in one spot, cheese and lettuce and tomato in another, and hamburger patties in the middle. They were thick and juicy and nearly black from the grill.

They looked good. *Really* good.

The problem wasn't that they made Rylie's mouth water, even though she wanted to stay a vegetarian. The problem was that she wished they were bloodier.

"Better a steak than a fawn," she muttered to herself, taking three hamburger patties back to her table.

Rylie stared at the contents of her plate. Cows had been farmed in a factory for these hamburgers, and it was wrong to eat animal flesh. The smell made her stomach growl.

She tore off a small piece of patty, shut her eyes, and ate.

Physically, it was easy to eat the hamburger. Her body longed for meat. Mentally, it was a little more complicated. She couldn't help but think of the pretty calves with long eyelashes near her aunt's ranch in Colorado. But it was, as Seth said, easier than killing something with her teeth. She ate quickly and tried not to taste it.

The new moon sickness began creeping in not long after.

Rylie met Seth at the same place on the trail as last time. She felt queasy and weak. The hike out that far made her tired. "Where are we going?" she asked as he led her into the forest.

"You'll see. I found a safe place."

She was trembling by the time they reached the clearing high on the mountain. Her skin was hot, and her sweat was cold in the warm breeze. She wished desperately for a jacket, or a cold swim, or *anything* to make her feel better.

The clearing was dotted with crumbling pieces of foundation. It was fenced off by low barbed wire, and signs had been posted to forbid trespass. Seth draped his bag over the fence so they could climb over safely.

Dozens of ruined buildings stood in the middle of the forest, but only one structure remained intact: a gray stone box barely bigger than Rylie's cabin. Parts of the roof had collapsed, letting starlight illuminate the dark innards of the building. Seth set a lantern on the edge of what might have once been a stone bench.

"This place looks old," Rylie said, hanging by the doorway.

"It's the remnants of a settler outpost. There used to be a lot more. The stone for this building was quarried from Gray Mountain itself, which is why it's survived so long."

Seth looped long, thick ropes around his arms and removed chains from his bags. They were meant for Rylie. She felt sick watching him work.

She wandered along the walls to distract herself, gazing up at the boarded windows. There were still a couple pieces of stained glass in the narrow frames. Rylie traced her fingers along the warped, bubbled windows. It hinted at beautiful art that had long since been destroyed.

Shifting through some of the rubble, she found two pieces of brass that looked like they had once been bound together. When she held them so the grooves aligned, they formed a cross. "Was this a church?"

"I think so," he said.

"What destroyed it?"

"Time," Seth said, dropping the chains on the floor. Metal rang against stone. "And an attack. They fortified this building as a safe haven against werewolves and other animal spirits. The log cabins were easy to break or burn, so this was their fortress." He fixed one end of the chain to a bracket on the wall. "I think they bound werewolves in here for questioning. It should be strong enough for you."

Rylie swallowed hard. She was going to be tied up somewhere other werewolves had been tortured in the past. It was almost enough to make her back out.

"And this is something you read in another book of yours," she said. Seth didn't respond. "Where did you find this stuff?"

"They used to offer rock climbing at Golden Lake until there were too many accidents. The storage sheds still had all the equipment for it. Try to break this." He offered her one end of the chain.

"Are you kidding?"

"You're a lot stronger than you used to be," Seth said.

Rylie wrapped the chain around her forearm, gripping it hard, and yanked. The metal was securely moored in the wall and held firm.

Seth began harnessing Rylie using a combination of ropes, chains, and karabiners. She held her arms up so he could harness her chest and hips. By the time he was done, Rylie was restrained by ropes around the thighs and upper arms as well, connecting her to several of the metal rings.

He backed up to survey his work. "Does this hurt?"

Rylie shook her head, suppressing a fresh bout of chills. "Isn't this overkill? I get weak on the new moon."

"You got weak on the *last* new moon," he corrected.

He moved further away. She wished he would stay with her, but he needed to be out of arm's reach, especially if she got teeth and claws again. "What about the muzzle?"

"Do you want it?"

She took a deep breath and nodded. "I wouldn't have killed the fawn if I'd listened to you last time."

Seth tied it around Rylie's face. It hung loose in the front where her snout would elongate to fill it. He gave her a half-hearted smile and squeezed her hand before stepping away. Rylie didn't think she imagined his fingers lingering on hers.

"I'll be here the whole time. I won't go anywhere," he said, perching himself on the back of a pew.

Rylie sat on the ground to wait for the change. She couldn't find a comfortable position with all the chains restricting her movement. "I don't feel as sick as last time. Am I really going to turn again?"

Seth glanced at his watch. "Did you eat meat?" he asked. She nodded. "It makes it easier. You'll feel the moon's call soon."

He was right. Rylie shut her eyes and tried to brace herself against it, but she was too weak. There was no energy within her to struggle. The wolf rose from the depths of her mind. It wasn't as hungry and desperate as it had been on the full moon, and it felt almost as lethargic as she did.

"Don't watch me," she whispered to Seth. She wasn't sure if he obeyed.

This time, her fingers began to snap first. She dug her fingernails into her knee caps, gritting her teeth against the pain. When the claws began to bite into her skin, she clutched at the chains instead. Her claws made a metallic screech rubbing against them.

Her face began to fill the muzzle as her ears perked and slid up either side of her head. Blood throbbed through every pore of her skin.

The shrieks that came from her were neither animal nor human. She strained against the chains. The wolf twisted her legs until they were bloodied by the ropes. The metal rings in the walls creaked and groaned, but held firm.

Rylie's flesh itched and burned like a million bees swatted at her with razor wings. Fur tore from beneath her skin, sweeping from her shoulders to her hands and down her body. She was on fire and she couldn't escape it.

When all the changes were done, she slumped to the ground. The wolf felt weak and vulnerable lying on the floor of a human structure. She let out a whimper.

Something moved, and her eyes flew open.

A human stood overhead. He had captured her.

She threw herself against the ropes, snapping her teeth. The human's face was drawn and grim. He smelled of hunters—the kind of prey that tried to be predator. The kind of prey that might skin her for her pelt if given the chance. The wolf thrashed harder, but he didn't come within reach. He still had the faint, lingering odor of another wolf's pheromones on the bag at his feet.

"You're going to injure yourself struggling like that. I have something to help you relax and sleep tonight. I hope for your sake that you don't remember this tomorrow." Reaching into his bag, he removed a handful of shriveled blue flowers. The smell wafted over to her. It was vile. Sour. Toxic. The wolf let out a warning growl.

"It's aconite. Wolfsbane." He moved forward, crumbling the dried flowers in his palm.

One of his hands moved for her face. She jerked back, trying to bite him. Something held her jaw. The wolf rubbed her nose on the ground, trying to push it off with a hand. The human's shoved the powdered wolfsbane through the side of the muzzle, forcing it onto her tongue.

He withdrew his fingers and jumped back. The flower burned her mouth and throat. The wolf growled and whined, pulling harder at the ropes. It felt like acid creeping through her bones and melting away the tendons so she couldn't control herself.

Slowly, one muscle at a time, she relaxed. Her body slumped against the wall. Her eyes fell closed, and with a tiny whimper, she passed out. Seth watched her through the long night.

The dark moon crossed overhead unseen.

Thirteen

Trouble

Rylie felt awful the next morning. Seth didn't tell her why.

"Keep eating a lot of protein," he advised. "And try to get some sleep."

She managed the first instruction at breakfast that morning, devouring scrambled eggs and bacon by the dozen. Rylie was aware people were staring at her—Louise especially—but she was too hungry to be subtle. She started out by sneaking a spoonful of eggs, but she went back for seconds, and then thirds. Finally, she loaded a plate with nothing but thick slices of ham, bacon, and eggs, and devoured it without bothering to sit.

"Did you enjoy breakfast?" Louise asked as they walked toward the field where they would be having a scavenger hunt.

Rylie didn't respond. It was hard to be hung up on the nagging thoughts of all the pig she had just eaten when the wolf inside was practically purring with contentment—not that wolves purred.

Getting sleep was much harder. Rylie daydreamed of the comfort of her cot all day, but as soon as she lay down, her racing mind refused to let her sleep. She stared at the ceiling's wooden beams until they were touched by the morning light and dragged herself out of bed to stumble through another day.

When she got back the next evening, though, she didn't immediately climb into bed.

Something was different.

It wasn't that anything was misplaced, other than Byron the Destructor tipped on his side. Rylie sniffed the air.

Someone had been there. She could smell the oils from their skin on her clothes, the individual strands of hair that had drifted to the floor as they picked through her belongings and replaced them exactly as they had been before. Bending to put her nose close to the drawers, she could just make out the odor of their sweat.

She had smelled this at the boy's side of camp. It was the werewolf in human form. It had been searching through her belongings, but for what?

Rylie had to tell Seth.

She immediately wrote a note on a clean journal page: *The werewolf was here. We have to talk.* She wedged the paper in her window like usual, and waited.

And waited.

Seth didn't arrive to take the note that night. She fell asleep shortly before dawn and woke up to find the note still in place.

Rylie stood outside the cabin while everyone else showered, staring into the forest. Was the werewolf still watching her? Was it out amongst the trees, waiting to see how she would react to the invasion?

She took deep, even breaths, letting her eyes fall closed so her sight wouldn't distract her. After a moment, she found the lingering smell of the werewolf. It wasn't far away—too far to see, but with the wind going just the right way, close enough to detect. It had moved through camp the night before, and the day before that. It might have been lurking nearby for days.

Now that Rylie knew what to look for, the range of scents painted a colorful picture in her mind. The wolf had mud on its feet from the dark, shady places much higher on the mountain where snow never melted. The cold bite of winter lingered on the edges of the summer shrubs. She even picked up musty old stone quarried from the mountain, and rusty chains.

The werewolf had been to the same ruins as Rylie.

"Who are you?" she whispered as though it would hear her and respond.

Rylie could tell the werewolf had paid special attention to her books. They smelled the strongest. It had even examined The Legends of Gray Mountain, but it left the folder. The werewolf wasn't looking for that. What did it want?

Her journal. The werewolf wanted her journal. It was never left amongst her belongings, not since Amber and Patricia had read it. Maybe it was trying to confirm Rylie had begun to change.

She ran her nose over the pages of The Legends. Breathing in again and again, savoring the woodsy musk, Rylie memorized the werewolf's smell. In human form, she needed to concentrate to differentiate smells, but she would remember it next time she changed.

She could track the werewolf to its den.

Checking the seam of her window, Rylie found the note to Seth where she left it. She didn't want to wait anymore. The werewolf was getting closer, and she had to talk to him.

Rylie and Seth needed to move against the werewolf.

She spent the day trying to decide how to reach Seth. The hike over to Golden Lake was long, and Rylie wasn't sure she could make it there and back between Louise's checks on the cabin. She also didn't have a canoe or any way into the supply shed to borrow one.

The counselor's ATVs caught her eye on the way to dinner, and an idea blossomed.

Rylie caught up with Louise after they ate. "How long have you been a counselor here?" she asked casually.

"I've done this every summer since I graduated high school," she said, "so this is my fifth year. It's a great summer job. It's helped put me through college."

"That's cool." A thought occurred to her. "Do you know much about the history of the two camps?"

"Yes, actually, I do! I got my undergraduate degree in anthropology." Louise turned to take the path toward Group B's campsite, and Rylie followed. "My specialty was legends and mythology. I'm going to South America to work on my graduate degree this fall. Are you interested in that kind of thing?"

"Yeah," Rylie said. "I'm especially interested in the settlers that originally lived on Gray Mountain."

"Those are pretty good stories. Very dark, though. Bloody."

She gave a weak smile. "That's what makes it cool."

"What have you heard about the local legends?"

Way too much, Rylie thought bitterly. "I heard the original settlers fought a war against the animal spirits of the forest."

"That's the story. This land was supposed to be sacred to the gods of the beasts," Louise said.

"What made it sacred?"

"You notice how tall some of these peaks are?" She pointed up at the mountain. Even though the camp was already high on its face, Gray Mountain stretched much taller. "The gods were believed to live on the moon. They said the animals would climb to the top to commune with the gods and find out how to best serve them. This was also how the gods got to Earth. They only had to take a step down."

"Why did the settlers think that?" Rylie asked.

"There's supposed to be some pretty cool natural rock formations on the highest peak. I've heard they look like a temple, but I haven't hiked that far," Louise said.

"And that's where the animals talk to their moon gods."

"Supposedly. That's why they thought the wolves howled so loud here."

"What about the curse?" Rylie asked. When Louise looked confused, she went on. "The curse that turned the settlers into wolves."

"Oh. That's not how I heard the legend. The werewolf thing—that was a deal between the humans and the animal gods. It was a blessing meant to bring man and nature together. It ended the war."

"How could transforming into a monster be a blessing?"

"Wolves aren't monsters," Louise said. "They're extremely intelligent."

"Right. So how did the legends say you could lift the 'blessing' of the animal gods?"

The counselor laughed. "I have no idea. It's just myth! Superstition! Anyone moving into the wild frontier would have had problems with the environment. Living on Gray Mountain was rough and the settlers had wild imaginations. The fact that no native tribes lived here only added fuel to the fire."

"I guess," Rylie said, disappointed. They reached the camp, and Louise moved to go to her cabin. Rylie stopped her. "Hey Louise?"

"Yes?"

"Can I... have a hug?"

Louise smiled. "Of course."

They embraced. Rylie was careful not to squeeze hard enough to hurt the counselor. Louise walked away grinning, and Rylie waited until she was gone to look down at her hand. She had slipped the black key off Louise's keychain.

She was sure it went to the all-terrain vehicles parked by the office.

Rylie snuck out after curfew, taking no flashlights or maps. She had to trust that she could find her way to the other side by smell.

But the key didn't work on any of the ATVs.

She frowned at the key in her hand. It looked like a car key. If it wasn't for the ATVs, then what *was* it for?

Something shiny and black caught her eye around the side of the shed. It was an SUV the counselors and administrators used to get from Golden Lake to Silver Brook, and it was brand new. It wasn't even muddy.

Holding her breath, Rylie tried the key on the driver's door. It unlocked.

She grinned.

Five minutes later, she was roaring along the rail, gripping the steering wheel with shaking hands. There was a lot of power in the SUV's engine. It was a beast on the steep trail.

Rylie didn't have her learning permit, much less her driver's license. She had only driven her dad's tiny old sedan before. This thing was much bigger, and much more powerful, than anything she had ever controlled in her life. Every little movement of the steering wheel made it swerve like crazy.

Her heart pounding, she gripped the wheel as hard as she could and tried not to flip the SUV. It bounced over every rock and dip. The headlights swayed over the road.

When hiking, the trip around the lake was supposed to take three or four hours. Even with Rylie's cautious driving, though, it took less than an hour for her to reach the "Welcome to Camp Golden Lake!" sign. She braked a little too suddenly, and the SUV stopped with a jerk.

Rylie's legs trembled as she climbed out of the car to look at the sign, dizzy with adrenaline. She had to stop and brace her hands her hands against her knees. "Oh my God," she whispered. Driving was *awesome*.

A map of the camp was mounted beside the welcome sign. It looked like Golden Lake was laid out almost like a mirror of Silver Brook, but the map was useless without knowing Seth's cabin number.

After all that effort to steal the SUV and sneak over to camp, Rylie had no idea where she was going.

Five camps, with five cabins each. What else could Rylie do? She would have to look around and hope Seth was awake. She turned to get back in the driver's seat.

A hand clamped down on Rylie's elbow. She shrieked.

"I'm surprised you came back," Jericho said, towering over her like a furious storm cloud. "I didn't think you would be that stupid."

He jerked her away from the SUV. "No!" Rylie cried.

She thought she saw Seth standing out amongst the trees before Jericho hauled her to the office, but it didn't matter. Rylie had already been caught.

• ◯ •

Rylie sat on a chair by the door of the director's office, staring at her hands as she waited for the verdict.

Jericho and Louise had been in a phone meeting with Jessica and the director for the last two hours. She wasn't optimistic about her punishment. Rylie had finally found the end of Louise's patience. She had been furious when Jericho woke her up at midnight to discover Rylie had stolen her key.

Going over to the side of the lake was a minor infraction. It was banned, but a few kids dared to do it a couple times every summer. A fifteen year old stealing the counselors' SUV to drive to the opposite side, however, wasn't just banned. It was illegal.

She would bet anything that Jericho was rooting for her arrest. Jessica was probably her only chance now, and that wasn't saying much. She already wanted Rylie to come home.

Rylie felt sick. Horrible visions of transforming into a werewolf at her mom's condo swam through her mind. What if she destroyed the building? Worse, what if she ate her mom?

And what if she never saw Seth again?

Louise emerged from the office. Rylie stood up.

"Am I…?" she asked.

"You can stay."

Relief flooded Rylie, and it was so overwhelming that her knees buckled. She caught herself on the back of the chair. "Thank you."

Louise wasn't smiling. "I defended you in there. If Jericho and I hadn't begged them to let you stay, you would be going home right now."

"Jericho stood up for me?"

"You could be going home in *handcuffs*. You stole my key. You stole the SUV. You went to the other side of the lake, where girls aren't allowed." She threw her hands in the air. "Jesus, Rylie! What were you thinking?"

"I know you won't believe me, but I had to do it," Rylie said. "Please, Louise."

"I've bent over backwards to help you, but this is it. I'm drawing the line here. You've betrayed my trust, and I can't deal with you anymore."

Louise's rejection stung worse than Rylie expected. "I had to do it," she repeated in a tiny voice.

"You're getting moved to another group for the rest of the summer. Group E has more counselors, and one of them is always awake at night so you can be supervised. Katie's going to take you to your new cabin."

"I'm sorry," Rylie said.

"You're confined to the cabin for the next week. You can only leave for showers and meals. The director will reevaluate if you should be allowed to participate in the last two weeks of camp after that."

"Confined? I can't be confined!"

"This is what you wanted, and you got it," Louise said, her eyes red and shining. "Congratulations."

She walked out without giving Rylie a second look.

Fourteen

Confinement

Rylie's new roommates were much friendlier than her old ones, but this time, she had no loft to convert into her private bedroom. The cabin only had three beds, one on each wall. The other two were occupied by girls who had gotten in trouble earlier in the summer.

"What did *you* do?" asked a brunette named Gina.

"I stole a car to go to the other camp," Rylie said. "You?"

"I hit a girl in the showers." She grinned. "Then Nancy and I jumped her behind the nurse's office." Nancy was grinning, too. Neither of them looked like they felt bad about it, so Rylie decided to leave them alone.

They weren't confined to the cabin like Rylie. Gina and Nancy got to participate in group activities while she wrote in her journal. It was boring and lonely, and Katie checked on her every hour or two. There was never a chance to sneak out.

The back window to the cabin slipped open on the third day of her confinement. Seth climbed in.

"Where have you been?" Rylie hissed. "I've been trying to get a hold of you for ages!"

"I've been at Golden Lake. I'm being watched, so I couldn't get away. It was hard to find you."

"Well, I'm never getting away again! I'm under constant surveillance now."

"You can't change inside the cabin," Seth said. "Especially not on a full moon. You could kill the other campers. Not to mention it would raise a few awkward questions."

Rylie had already considered that. It had been the subject of her nightmares the night before. "I know. Plus, I think the other werewolf has been looking for me. It went through my stuff twice. It knows who I am."

"What do you think it wants?"

"I don't know," she said, "but I think we can figure out who it is. It left its scent all over when it went through my stuff this time, so I think I can track it when I change this time. We can figure out where it's spending the moons."

A smile appeared on Seth's face. "Excellent. But that will mean letting you run loose."

"I can control myself." Rylie made herself sound brave and confident, even though she didn't feel it. The wolf was nuts. It would go after the other werewolf if she could smell it, but she had no way to keep herself from attacking any unlucky human that might cross her path.

Seth didn't seem worried. "We'll have to figure out how to sneak you out. Do you have any friends here? Anyone who can distract the counselor on duty?"

Rylie didn't even have to think about it. "Yeah." Cassidy would love to help her get into trouble. The trick would be getting to talk to her before the full moon—she was confined for the rest of the week, and the full moon was in two days. "I don't know when we can talk. I used to see her at meals, but our eating times are different now I'm in this group."

"Do you guys have weekly campfire announcements, like at Golden Lake?" he asked. "The other camp is having theirs tomorrow. That would be perfect."

"You're right." Rylie glanced at the door. "You need to get out of here before you get caught. If Katie sees you, we're both dead."

"Okay." He pushed the window open again. "I'm sorry I didn't get to you sooner."

Seth departed, leaving Rylie to sit alone and think about the full moon.

The bonfire announcements weren't considered a "fun" activity, so Rylie was allowed to attend. She gave Katie the slip amongst the gathering crowd and sought out Cassidy, who had already found a seat on one of the highest benches.

"I'm surprised you're here," Cassidy said as Rylie sat beside her. "I hear you're confined to your cabin."

"The rumors are true," she said grimly.

"Everyone be quiet!" the director called, holding up both hands to silence the campers.

Most of the talking died off, but Rylie leaned close to Cassidy's ear. She could see Katie looking for her near the fire, so there wasn't much time. "I need to sneak out of camp tomorrow night," she whispered.

Cassidy's eyes lit up. "Really? Why?"

"I'm meeting a guy, but I'm under constant surveillance. I need someone to…" Rylie fell silent as another counselor passed, waiting to continue until she was gone. "I need someone to distract the counselor on duty so I can sneak out after curfew and get back in at dawn. You're not far from me. Do you think…?"

"That sounds like fun," Cassidy said, grinning. "Who's this guy you're sneaking out to meet?"

Rylie pushed a pebble around with the toe of her hiking boots. "His name is Seth. He's from Golden Lake."

"Is he cute?"

She thought of his muscular shoulders and slanted smile, and her cheeks got hot. "Oh yeah. Really cute."

"Be careful," Cassidy warned. "Is this guy worth the trouble?"

"Definitely."

She shrugged. "Your choice. I'll totally help."

The activity director's voice caught Rylie's ear. "There's going to be a cross-camp social event in a week. Everyone from our side and the boys' side will attend," the director said. "It used to be a yearly tradition, but we stopped about seven years ago after things got a little out of hand." Rylie felt a little thrill. The boys from Camp Golden Lake included Seth. "There will be music, dancing, and food. It's a great time to meet our brothers from the other camp."

"And hook up with hotties you've been sneaking out to bang," Cassidy whispered, nudging her elbow in Rylie's side.

Her cheeks heated. "Sure, if I'm allowed to go."

"Wear your nicest hiking boots!" joked the director. Everyone laughed.

Katie caught up with Rylie when everyone stood to go to dinner. She didn't bother chastising Rylie for sneaking off, but she hovered behind her as they walked to the mess like a body guard. "Hey Katie," Rylie said. "I was thinking... since I'm going to be off cabin restriction by then... will I get to go to the dance?"

Her eyes narrowed. "No, I don't think so. I'll stay back at camp with you."

"Please? I can't miss the dance!"

"You got caught trying to meet a boy over there. It's not a punishment if we let you meet him. Okay? I don't want to hear about it."

"But that's not fair!" Rylie complained. She never got to see Seth unless something was wrong. She wanted one chance to have fun before the summer ended. Her chin quivered as she tried not to cry. "Everyone else gets to go!"

"I told you, I don't want to hear it. Go eat dinner."

Fifteen

Sacred Ground

Cassidy and Rylie agreed on how she could sneak out while roasting marshmallows after dinner. Their plans were simple enough, but Rylie spent the next couple of days worrying anyway. Katie was sharp. If Cassidy didn't keep her promise, there was no way Rylie could escape.

After curfew on the full moon, Rylie lay nervously in bed with her window open and her hiking boots laced. She listened to the breeze outside and her roommates' snoring.

Her stomach was heavy with all the meat she had eaten in the hopes the wolf would be satiated enough not to attack another deer. She had also taken deep sniffs of her books again to get the werewolf's scent fresh in her nose. Rylie could even detect it on the air as a human.

The minutes crawled by. Rylie waited, skin crawling, for Cassidy to arrive.

Fortunately, she was as good as her word. Shortly after the wall clock clicked over to ten, she heard Katie speak outside. "Hey! You there! What are you doing out of bed?"

That was her cue. Rylie clambered out the window and peered around the cabin. Katie had been seated so she could watch Rylie's door, but now her back was turned. She was calling to Cassidy in the trees.

"Oh no, I must have gotten lost," Cassidy said, sounding so innocent that it had to be obvious she was up to something. She was in her pajamas and scrubbing at her face sleepily. "I'm with Group D and I was looking for the bathrooms. Which camp is this?"

Katie walked over to talk to her, and Rylie darted across the clearing, hanging low to the ground. Her heart pounded. She was sure Katie would spot her at any moment, but she made it to the trail without being followed.

"Thank you, Cassidy," Rylie whispered. She couldn't wait to see how her friend distracted the counselor first thing in the morning. The bathroom excuse couldn't work twice.

Rylie and Seth met at their usual spot. He didn't have his bag of tricks this time. The only thing Seth brought was a belt knife as long as his forearm. He looked ready to move fast, but Rylie wondered if that would be enough to keep up with her on the loose.

"Let's hike as far as we can before you change," Seth suggested. "Wherever the werewolf made its den, it must be a long way from camp."

They walked through the forest, straying off the trail when they approached the place Rylie had been attacked. "There's going to be a camp social between the girl's side of the lake and the boy's side," she said, pretending to be concentrating on climbing a pile of boulders. It was actually so easy now she could have done it upside down and backwards. "Have you heard about it?"

"We haven't had announcements this week yet."

"It sounds like all the girls are going to get bused over to Golden Lake. I guess there's going to be dancing and stuff." She tried to sound casual. "It kind of sounds like fun."

Seth made a face. "I don't dance."

"Oh."

"But I might dance with you," he said. His shoulder bumped hers.

Her cheeks got hot. There was nothing romantic about sneaking into the forest so she could safely become a half-monster, but she almost forgot about it in that moment. "So you're going to go?"

"Maybe, if you're coming."

"I want to. I don't know. The stupid counselor they have watching me doesn't think I should get to have any fun."

"Go over her head," he suggested. "Ask the director."

"That might not help. Everyone's still pretty mad at me," Rylie said.

Seth gave her his slanted smile, and her heart beat a little faster. "I hope you can go."

She didn't have time to get excited. The moon began to call as it rose higher in the sky. After her last several transformations, she could recognize the creeping feeling that meant she was running out of time as a human. It was happening earlier than ever before. "I think I'm going to change."

Seth stopped. The forest was thick and secluded, so it was as good a place as any.

"Okay. You should get ready," he said.

"Get ready?"

"You're going to be almost entirely wolf this time. You probably won't be able to fit into your clothes anymore."

Rylie blushed. "Right."

"I'll go over there while you change." Seth pointed to a ridge not far above them. "I won't look, I promise. Once you pick up the werewolf's smell, I'll follow."

"I don't think I can make myself wait for you to catch up with me," Rylie warned.

He laughed. "Don't worry. I can keep up."

"Okay. I'll see you on the other side."

Seth dissolved into the trees, and Rylie went about the business of getting undressed and stashing her clothes behind a bush. She should have felt weird getting naked in such an open area. Rylie was modest—she didn't even wear bikinis to the beach. But it felt completely normal to be bare-fleshed in the forest.

She could hear Seth climbing the ridge. Even if she felt normal being naked, she was still blushing. She felt like she might blush for the rest of her life.

The moon called to her, drawing the beast out. She tried to focus on staying human as long as she could. She visualized her human fingers and toes, her face, her blonde hair. But there was no fighting it. The curse was too powerful.

She changed fast this time, as though her body was beginning to remember the form. Rylie cried out as her face stretched. Her spine elongated into a tail, and her skin burned as fur grew. The only difference this time was that her knees snapped and reversed, forcing her onto all four legs.

The wolf didn't care about the pain. Rylie was grateful when it took over for her.

She focused on the smell of the werewolf when her sharpened senses came to life. Although she couldn't remember why she recognized the smell, she knew she needed to follow it. Locating the other beast was the only way she could secure her territory.

Nose to the air, she tracked the smell across the trail and higher into the mountain. She didn't notice the human trying to follow her.

The wolf paused by a tree and smelled it. Tufts of fur were stuck to the rough bark, giving her a fresh whiff of the werewolf's smell. It was recent. He was near.

Twigs cracked behind her. She turned and saw nothing.

Quickening her pace, she grew more excited as the scent became fresher. It was still at least an hour's run ahead, but she was gaining on it.

The wind shifted, blowing the smell of a human in her direction. This time, when she looked behind her, she saw him struggling to keep up with her. In the back of her mind, Rylie worried for Seth. The wolf was only impressed that he managed to follow her for so long.

But she also didn't want anything tracking her. She began to run, leaping from rock to rock.

"Rylie!" yelled the human.

She paid him no mind. There was no way he could keep up with her as she approached the steeper places on the mountain. For half an hour, she ran, tracking the passage of night by the moon's march across the sky.

When the moon reached its apex, she looked behind her again. There was no sign of the human. She had lost him. Rylie gave a small, inward cry of disappointment.

The wolf's pulse sped. The scent she was tracking grew stronger, and she hurried to catch up with it. She crossed the river, jumping over a natural bridge created by a toppled tree. At long last, the trees disappeared entirely, replaced by rough rock worn smooth by the wind.

The smell had vanished.

She stopped, looking around in confusion. She was certain she hadn't left the territory, so the werewolf should have been nearby.

Proceeding with her nose to the ground, she searched for the smell once more. The wolf had almost reached the very top of Gray Mountain. All the other mountains fell away beneath her as she climbed.

And then she reached the peak.

Natural stone pillars formed a ring on a smooth, open plane at the top. It was the same gray stone as the ruins of the church, and it gave off the same air of being holy land: eerily quiet, untouched by wind, and empty of all the little animals that lived elsewhere on Gray Mountain. Snow dotted the shadowy places beneath the rocks where it would never melt, even on the hottest days of summer. Ice limned the pillars. Her breath came from her in cloudy puffs.

No sound broke the silence but her padding feet. But while it was quiet, the litany of smells formed brilliant images in her mind of men and beasts, and creatures in between. It was as though hundreds of years of smells lingered in one place.

She climbed a sloped rock that stood above the others. The moon was so huge it looked like she could have leapt onto its surface.

While sitting back on her haunches, the wolf was the tallest point around. The mountain range stretched below her for miles in every direction, and the trees looked like nothing more than distant grass. Tiny pinpoints of light marked the human outposts below.

The wolf tilted her head back and gave a soft howl to the swollen moon.

Another howl responded.

She wasn't alone.

Looking down upon the rocks below, she saw an animal circling its way up the mountain. It was not a wolf of the forest, of the earth and trees and dark dens. She could smell man on its thick fur and the sour tang of its cursed saliva.

She moved down the rocks. It was not a safe position, and she wanted to be ready to fight.

It approached her. She gave a small warning growl.

They stood across from each other at the apex of the mountain, backed by nothing but the clear sky and moon. She puffed herself up to look more intimidating. The wolf knew she was not complete yet, so the werewolf was stronger. She would not show weakness.

A second dark shape moved between the rocks, emerging in the moonlight.

Two werewolves.

Blood formed a mask on the face of the smaller beast. It had been eating something. They both seemed familiar in some way, as though they were pack—but she had no pack. The wolf was alone.

They growled and circled her. She stood her ground, turning to keep them in her line of sight.

She was smaller than both of them, still half-human. The two werewolves were massive beasts, almost more demon than wolf, with bulky shoulders and paws the size of boulders. Their teeth and claws were silver knives in the moonlight. She couldn't take either of them alone, much less both.

The bigger werewolf moved forward to sniff her, and its nose raked over her shoulders and back. This was not the one who had been in her home. This was the one that had bitten her. Her upper lip skinned over her teeth.

Tension throbbed in the air between them. The bigger werewolf stepped back, and the smaller darted at her heels, snapping its teeth.

She growled and lunged, striking the small werewolf in the side. They rolled together across the mountain and struck one of the rock pillars. She leapt off. It tried to bury its jaws in her belly, and she dodged back.

The big werewolf tried to move between them, but she wouldn't give it a chance. Her teeth sank into the furred ruff around its neck. It yelped.

Pain flashed across her side as the smaller one clawed her ribs. Blood spurted from her fur.

She was outmatched two to one, and both were more powerful. One injury was enough to convince her that the fight wasn't worth it. Turning, she fled down the mountain.

They followed.

The wolf's paws pounded against rock. She wanted to reach the trees to hide, but the flash of intelligence that was

Rylie told her it wouldn't be good enough. She needed to make them lose her scent.

She ducked when the smaller one leapt again, and she felt the breeze from its passing ruffle her fur. It landed in front of her. She swerved to avoid it.

A splashing sound reached her ears across the crisp, empty night air. The river. Rylie could use it to mask her smell.

Angling south, she put on a burst of speed. The werewolves growled and snapped and drooled behind her. They weren't just stronger; they were faster too. She felt jaws bite at her tail, and she tucked it between her legs to keep it out of reach.

The mountain grew steep. She lost her footing on gravel and slid, paws scrabbling wildly for purchase.

She bounced on the rocks and landed in a cluster of trees with a crunch. The branches battered her body, scraping and catching on her fine fur. A thick bough connected with her stomach. She grunted and slipped to the ground below.

Her pursuers were nowhere in sight, but she could hear them. The werewolves crashed thunderously through the branches. There was no time to lick her injuries even though she was half-skinned from her slide down the rocks.

Getting back to her paws, she dove for the river.

It split into many smaller brooks by the camp, but it ran thick and furious in the mountains. The last of the melting ice and snow turned it into a freezing, foamy spray. Perfect.

The bigger werewolf burst from the trees in front of her. She barely stopped herself in time, digging her claws into the ground. She turned to run the other way, but the smaller werewolf blocked her.

She hunched her shoulders and growled. They didn't look threatened.

So close to the river. So close to safety. Rylie was screaming inside.

The two werewolves maneuvered to force her backward toward a steep drop off. The wolf tried to hold her ground on the very edge.

Glancing down, she saw the river far below. It was a waterfall.

She looked between the werewolves and the river. It was a creature of instinct, and not decision-making; the beast had no means to decide whether potential death by falling or drowning was better than being torn apart at the jaws of certain death.

But Rylie knew she didn't want to be eaten. The smaller werewolf darted forward.

Rylie threw herself off the waterfall.

She hit the water. All the air rushed out of her with a shock of pain. She was swept downriver instantly, battered by rocks and crashing rapids.

The wolf struggled to surface for air. Her nose found oxygen for a brief second, but then she sank below again. There was no up or down in the river. There was only chaos and the struggle of trying to paddle toward the shore.

Something hard hit her, tearing open the wound on her side afresh. The wolf gasped and sucked in water. She caught on a boulder and the river crushed her to its side.

Her snout pushed into the air. She breathed fresh air for a moment, then was swept away once more.

Beyond the row of boulders, the river grew calmer. She didn't have to fight to float at the surface. She sped down the mountain, unable to do anything but keep breathing and let the water take her away.

Her paws finally found purchase in the mud. Her rapid descent halted.

Inch by inch, the wolf dredged herself out of the water, fur heavy with moisture. It doubled her weight. Finally, she collapsed on dry land.

Coughing up a lungful of fluid, she tried to make sense of her surroundings. Was she safe? The shore was near where she had begun the night. It saved her hours of walking, but now she was wet and cold and broken from hitting the rocks on the way down.

Shaking out her fur, she stood on wobbling legs and forced her weary body to trot away from the river. She kept her ears perked, but she couldn't hear the werewolves following.

She continued until she grew too tired, then curled up in the shelter of thick bushes to rest. The wolf sniffed the air, but there was nothing to smell. They had not followed her. The only werewolf scents were hours old.

Licking the wound on her side, she cleaned grit and hair from her lesions so they could heal. Blood dribbled across the ground. A fever swept over her beneath the chill of her damp fur. Once she could rest, the wounds would disappear.

Morning approached slowly, and the wolf curled her tail over her nose to doze. The beast didn't dream.

Something in the back of her mind nudged at her when the first rays of sunlight touched the air, stirring her from her rest. Taking deep sniffs of the ground, a different scent caught her attention. It was a familiar, human smell. She snuffled through the bushes and found a folded pile of clothing.

Rylie. These clothes belonged to Rylie. The wolf's mind faded away with the smell of her human form.

Dawn crept into the sky, turning the violet air into gold. A beam of light touched her through the trees.

Fire swept over her skin as all her fur fell to the forest floor, leaving bare flesh behind. Stinging pains pricked her jaw as her snout receded into a normal chin and nose. Her gums bled as her sharp teeth fell out and the blunt human teeth grew in their place.

Rylie found herself lying naked on the dirt with pine needles stabbing her in the side. She sat up, looking at herself in confusion.

Why was she naked outside?

She tried to remember the night before, but she couldn't recall anything. Rylie knew she had hiked up the mountain with Seth, and that they intended to track the werewolf, but things were all a blur from there.

"Seth?" she called. No response. They must have been separated.

Blood soaked into the ground around her, and Rylie suspected it was hers. She felt hot and itchy like she always did after super-healing. No injuries remained upon inspection, but her hair was strangely damp.

Rylie felt there was something very, very important she needed to warn Seth about, but it was as though the wolf was someone else even though they occupied the same body. She didn't have access to its memories.

The sky grew lighter. It wouldn't be long before Katie checked her cabin.

Dressing quickly, she ran down the mountain to the trail, hoping Cassidy would be where she said she would.

It was even more dangerous trying to sneak back into camp than it was sneaking out. At least at the beginning of the night, it had been dark.

But Cassidy wasn't waiting at the mouth of camp.

Rylie waited a few minutes. As the time for cabin checks inched closer, she grew more impatient. Her friend must have fallen asleep.

There was no other option: she had to sneak in.

Angling herself so she would enter from the back, Rylie picked her way through the trees. Hopefully none of her roommates had gotten cold and shut the window. Then she would *really* be in trouble.

Rylie heard shouting. "Louise! Over here!" It was Katie.

Her stomach turned. Had they seen her?

She hid behind a tree and peered around the side. Katie, Louise, and a pair of counselors she didn't recognize were hurrying up the trail in the opposite direction. They carried flashlights to brighten the dim morning.

It was the perfect distraction, but Rylie couldn't resist. She had to see what was so exciting.

Following them from a safe distance, she saw the counselors stop off the side of the trail. Rylie vaguely recalled passing through this area the night before.

"What happened?" Louise asked. Her voice was tight.

"Meredith found her this morning. We think it was an animal attack."

"Is she…?"

"Yeah. She's dead," Katie said.

Dead? Rylie strained to see who they were talking about.

She caught a glimpse of a gold anklet, and her stomach flipped. "Oh my God," Rylie whispered.

She tried to run, but she only got three steps before collapsing. Her stomach heaved. Rylie vomited her dinner into the bushes.

It wasn't just any body. It was Amber.

Sixteen

The Camp Social

News of Amber's death spread quickly.

It was impossible to hide the arrival of police and park rangers. They came in with blaring sirens. Ambulances, photographers, and a whole mess of other officials arrived to mark lines on the trail, collect evidence, and analyze the body. The counselors tried to keep everyone away, but a few girls managed to sneak in anyway.

By the time the police cleaned up and left in the evening, everyone knew what happened.

Rylie had no problems getting back into her cabin unseen. The counselors didn't even retrieve the campers for showers. When everyone else went to breakfast, she sat on the edge of her bed and tried to remember, rapping her journaling pen against her knee.

She had glimpsed Amber's injuries. It had not been a random animal attack: Amber had been killed by a werewolf.

The question was… had Rylie been the one to do it?

She stared out at the forest as she gnawed her bottom lip. She still hadn't shaken that nagging feeling that Seth needed to know something about the night before. Was it that she had attacked someone? *Killed* someone? Rylie hated Amber, but she didn't think she hated her that much.

What would Rylie's dad think of her if he knew his daughter might be a murderer? As much as it stung, she wondered if it was a mercy he hadn't lived to see her become a monster.

Nobody noticed Rylie's distraction. They were too busy talking about more interesting topics: what killed Amber, would it strike again, and was the camp getting closed?

"It was a bear," Katie said tersely when Rylie's roommates cornered her with questions at lights out. "The park rangers found it. They think it was fed by humans at their summer home far from here. This bear was caught in town twice already, so they put it to sleep this time. There's nothing to worry about."

"So the camp isn't closing?" Rylie asked, speaking up for the first time.

"No. The camp isn't closing. Now I'm going to turn off the lights and go to sleep, and if I hear you three talking, I'm signing you up to clean the bathrooms."

Her roommates, of course, sat up and began whispering as soon as the door shut. "Betty saw the body on her way back from the showers," Gina said.

Nancy pulled a face. "Ugh!"

"She said the body was torn into pieces. Isn't that sick?" Gina leaned toward Nancy's bed. "But the people in Group D don't think it was a bear."

"Then what?"

Gina lowered her voice into a dramatic undertone. "They said it was a monster."

Something rustled outside their door. They all jumped in unison—but Katie's voice called from outside. "I hope that's not talking I hear in there!"

"Shut up, guys," Rylie hissed. "I'm not cleaning the toilets." And the rumors were too close to reality for her liking.

New rules were enacted for the safety of the campers: No more going out alone at night to walk to the bathrooms. No groups smaller than three. Counselors had to escort girls everywhere. Any activities further away from Silver Brook than the outermost cabins were canceled for the rest of the summer, leaving everyone to do arts and crafts or sports.

Rylie was allowed to return to her activities, but since there was nothing fun going on, she spent her time the same way she had for the last week. She was getting toward the end of her journal, and didn't have much to write about. Instead, she worried about all the questions she had with no answers.

Most of all, she worried about the new moon.

Seth didn't visit her again, but he left little things on the windowsill that told Rylie he was around. Once it was a note—*I found an empty den while I was hiking, but no werewolves; I'll tell you if I learn anything*—and at other times, it was silly things, like an interesting rock he found in the forest and a drawing of the lake from the perspective of the boys' camp.

He even gave her a drawing of her eyes once. Rylie put it next to her bed and blushed every time she looked at it.

His gifts distracted her from thoughts of Amber and monsters. Rylie had to hide everything from her roommates to avoid questions, but she peeked at them in the drawer as often as possible.

The only thing more exciting to the campers than Amber's mauling was the upcoming dance party. Rylie watched Gina and Nancy prepare by tearing apart old clothes and sewing together new dresses using supplies from the arts and crafts room. There was plenty of time to get creative, now that nobody was hiking.

Rylie didn't join in. Katie had made it clear she wouldn't be going to the dance, so she could only hope that Seth would find time for a visit before the last moon.

"Have fun!" sang Gina as they headed for the buses.

Rylie gave her a weak wave. Fun. Of course. Sitting in her cabin while everyone else danced with boys would be so much *fun.*

After Gina and Nancy disappeared, she pulled out her journal to write. She had just laid her pen to the page when Katie stuck her head in, looking harried. "What are you doing? Aren't you going to get ready?"

"You said I'm not going."

"It's not safe for us to hang back at camp. We won't punish anyone by making them stay so we're a bigger group. Get dressed, because we're leaving in five minutes."

Rylie had never gotten ready as quickly as she did last night. She did her makeup in seconds, and she paired her nicest pair of capris with a loose white camisole. It wasn't as cute as she would have liked, but she hadn't packed expecting a date night.

Rylie was still trying to pin up her long blonde hair when Katie returned.

"We're leaving now. Come on."

Leaving her hair half-done, she followed Katie to the buses. The first one had already left. She jumped onto the last bus in the line and took a seat as it lurched forward. Her heart danced in her throat. Rylie was going to Camp Golden Lake. She was going to see Seth.

The road around the lake felt longer in the lumbering buses than it had during her mad dash in the SUV. It gave her plenty of time to finish her hair using a mirror begged off of Nancy. She wasn't the only one making last-minute preparations, either. All around her, girls were doing each other's makeup and adjusting their clothes.

"Listen up, ladies! We have a few ground rules," Katie called, standing in the aisle with her hands braced against the seats so she swayed with the movement of the bus. "In light of the bear problem, you're not allowed outside the recreation hall. There will be no inappropriate dancing and we'll clean up after ourselves." Giggles spread throughout the bus behind Rylie. They weren't giggling about having to clean up. "Tonight is special, so curfew is being put off a couple hours. We'll do a head count at eleven and board the buses to return. Remember, stay inside. It's for your safety."

The buses stopped to unload. Katie caught Rylie's elbow before she could jump out.

"Head count at *eleven*, Rylie."

She rolled her eyes. "I heard you the first time."

The boy's recreation hall was decorated like every school dance Rylie had been to. Fairy lights were wound around the exposed ceiling beams, and streamers were draped around the walls. A DJ's booth was set up on one side with the dance floor in the middle. Food had been laid out against the wall, but between nerves and Rylie's high-protein dinner (which had become a daily ritual), she had no appetite.

She stretched up on her toes and looked over the crowd, biting her lip. The room was kept in half-light, so it was hard to make faces out.

Seth was nowhere in sight. Rylie found an empty table and sat down. She swirled a little punch in the bottom of a cup, watching everyone around her. Patricia was two tables away. She looked like she wanted to dance even less than Rylie did. Her eyes were red and swollen, and Rylie felt a pang of sympathy.

Cassidy joined Rylie at the table. "Where's your hot boy?"

"I don't know. He's not here yet."

"Guess that means I've got you to myself," Cassidy said. "Want to dance?"

"Not really," Rylie said.

"What's the matter?"

My dad died, I might have killed Amber, and I haven't slept in weeks. "I wish Seth was here," she said. It wasn't exactly a lie. She changed subjects anyway. "What have you been up to?"

"Nothing, since they found Amber's body. Boring! Of course that dumb hag had to go making camp even worse by dying." Cassidy leaned toward her, a glint of interest in her eyes. "Isn't that scary? What do you think happened to her?"

"They said it was a bear."

"That's not what I heard. Rumor says…"

"The rumors are stupid. We're not in danger at some dance and I don't want to talk about it." She knew she sounded curt, but Rylie didn't care. Cassidy didn't seem bothered.

"You upset about it? I thought you hated Amber."

"I'm not mourning her, but she didn't deserve to die, either."

"She made your life miserable," Cassidy said. "Screw her. She wouldn't have cared if it was you."

Rylie finished off her punch and set the cup down. "Look, why don't you…?"

She saw a familiar face across the room and trailed off.

Seth emerged from the crowd, and Rylie had to remember how to breathe. He was wearing a black button-down shirt with narrow gray stripes and his hair was pulled into a short ponytail, showing off his dark eyes.

"Rylie," he greeted. "You look really good."

She blushed and stood. "Thanks."

Cassidy's mouth fell open. "*You're* Seth?"

"Oh, right. Seth, this is my friend Cassidy. Cassidy, this is… the boy." She added a significant tone to the last word. "I'll talk to you later, okay?"

Cassidy nodded mutely, and Rylie walked off with Seth.

"Let's go outside," he suggested, leaning in close so she could hear him over the music.

"We're not supposed to leave," she said.

"So what?"

Rylie laughed. "Good point."

After breaking into cabins in the middle of the night and sneaking around a werewolf-riddled forest, escaping the counselors to get outside wasn't exactly a challenge. He held her hand and pulled her toward the lake, and she giggled as she followed him down the path to the beach.

"It was too noisy in there to talk," Seth said. "Did I tell you I found the den? There were no signs of the werewolf now. I think it's moved on."

"Do we have to talk 'business'?" Rylie asked. "I'm almost out of time. I haven't thought about anything but monsters and my dad for... well, the whole summer." Her eyes stung, and she blinked away tears. "I just want to have fun, Seth. I don't want to think."

He gave her his sideways smile. "Then why don't we dance?"

"There's no music out here," Rylie said.

"That's fine." Seth wrapped his arms around her waist, and she settled hers on his shoulders. She couldn't repress a giggle. "What are you laughing at?"

"I feel silly."

Seth's eyes sparked. "You said you don't want to think about it, so just enjoy it."

Rylie gave him a mock-serious nod, and he spun her in his arms. They played more than danced, galloping across the sand in imitation of the tango and faking a jitterbug. Seth had a charming lack of rhythm, and she wasn't much better. They laughed together, splashing in the edge of the water and getting sand in their shoes.

It was more fun than she'd had all summer.

They ended up slow-dancing in the chilly shallows. Shutting her eyes, Rylie rested her cheek against his chest. They swayed to the beat of the lake and the wind in the trees, slowing until neither of them moved at all. She could hear his heartbeat and smell the leather on him even though he wasn't wearing his jacket. Rylie could have stayed there forever.

"What happens after the summer ends?" she asked. She didn't feel like giggling anymore.

He rested his chin on top of her head. "I don't know. The new moon is tomorrow. It won't be the same afterward."

"Will I be able to go to back to school?" Rylie wasn't really asking him. She knew the answer wouldn't have been good. Even if she survived the transformation on the new moon, she couldn't live with her mom in the city. It wasn't a safe place for a wild animal.

The truth was that Rylie had nowhere to go once camp ended. She could have worked something out with her dad, but he was gone now. Her mom would never understand.

After this, she would be alone.

Rylie sniffled. Seth's thumb brushed against her cheek, wiping away the tears. "It will all turn out fine," he said gently.

She looked up at him. The smile was gone. He was gazing at her very intently, his hair disappearing against the black sky above them. His hands tightened against the small of her back.

Rylie leaned toward him for a kiss.

Seth released her and ducked his head, turning away. "Look... I don't think we should do this."

Wounded, she stepped back. "Why?"

"I just don't think we should. Don't take it personally."

"What? You don't like me?" Her cheeks burned. "You've been sticking around even though I turn into this horrible *thing* every other week. You give me presents. You comforted me when my dad died. I thought... I mean..."

He walked away, rubbing the back of his neck. "I can't explain, okay? Please, Rylie."

Her eyes burned. The old Rylie, before several moons of transforming into a werewolf, would have nodded and left him alone. But now, anger burned in her chest, and a growl rose in her throat. "That's not good enough."

She turned and left. Seth called her, but didn't follow. "Rylie, come back here. Rylie!"

She ignored him. The rejection stung too badly.

Rylie didn't care who saw her storm across camp, reentering the recreation hall without watching for counselors. She was sure Katie and Louise must have seen, but before they could intercept her, she slammed into the bathroom.

Locking the door of a stall, she leaned against the divider and covered her face with her hands.

Stupid, stupid, stupid.

Of course he didn't like her. Why would he? He watched her kill a fawn with her teeth. Rylie barely even liked herself.

But he had been so nice to her all summer, and he was always there when she needed him. Then he took her dancing on the beach...

She sniffled and scrubbed the tears from her eyes with the heel of her hand. It didn't mean anything. Seth was being a good friend—Rylie's only real friend, as a matter of fact. It was stupid to try to kiss him. She wouldn't have survived the last several moons without his help, and she didn't stand a chance on the new moon without him, either.

Rylie needed him, and she had just driven him off. She had to get past her stupid feelings and apologize.

Jericho intercepted her before she could go out the back door again. "What are you doing?" he growled.

Rylie was too exhausted to argue with him. "I'm looking for someone."

"Who? Your little boyfriend?"

"Why do you care? I'm not doing anything wrong."

"As a matter of fact, you are," Jericho said. "All the campers have explicit instructions not to exit the building. It's for your safety."

"I need to find someone," she said, pushing past him. When he reached out a hand to stop her, Rylie tried to brush it aside. She was so strong that she expected to overpower him easily, but he didn't budge.

"I don't think so."

Rylie glared. "Fine. I'll wait for Seth to find me."

"Who?"

Realizing she had finally revealed his name, her mouth snapped shut. But rather than looking angry or delighted at hearing the name of Rylie's co-conspirator, Jericho looked confused.

"What is it?" she asked.

"There's nobody named Seth in the boys' camp," he said.

Her mouth fell open. Jericho was serious. "He's taller than me, and he has black hair, brown eyes, and tan skin. He's always dressed in black. You can't miss him."

Jericho's eyes narrowed. "You must be confused."

"I guess I must be," she said faintly. But if Seth wasn't from Camp Golden Lake, then who was he?

Seventeen

Hunter and Hunted

The night before the new moon found Rylie alone in her darkened cabin. The rest of the group was taking advantage of the moonless sky by learning about constellations, but Katie decided Rylie shouldn't participate in an activity where she could be out after the normal curfew.

"Go to bed," she had ordered, settling herself by the fire to whittle a piece of wood into a flute. Katie didn't make threats, but the image of her seated by the leaping flames with a knife was pretty convincing.

Rylie didn't argue. She was too scared anyway.

The new moon was coming.

She couldn't even make herself write in her journal. Rylie was going to have to face her first full transformation without Seth to help her, and she was out of time to find a cure. Even though the moon was barely a sliver in the sky, she could feel it pressing down on her as surely as though she carried its weight on her back.

The window creaked open. Seth climbed into the cabin dressed in his usual black shirt and jeans, and her heart jumped into her throat.

"What are you doing here?" Rylie asked, hugging her legs to her chest.

"I wanted to talk to you."

"No. I'm still being watched." She turned around so that her back faced him and rested her chin on top of her knees. "Go away."

"I don't care if it's dangerous. Rylie, look at me," Seth said, sitting next to her. She struggled to keep from crying again. It seemed like all she had been doing since her father's heart attack. "There's still a chance. You might not become a werewolf tomorrow."

That got her attention. "What? How? Did you find a cure?"

"It's not exactly a cure, but I know some people have been bitten and haven't changed."

Rylie finally looked at him. His expression was shuttered. Seth was hiding something. "Where did you hear that?"

"You know, my usual places," he said.

She finally snapped. "No, I don't know. How do *you* know so much? I read all of The Legends of Gray Mountain from back to front a hundred times and I never found half of what you've told me. You have another source."

"I told you I've read everything."

"You're lying to me," Rylie said. "I can smell it now." Her nose wrinkled. "That burned smell that follows you around—I've come across it before at my aunt's ranch in Colorado. I couldn't put a finger on it until I almost got mugged back home. It's gunpowder."

Seth reached for her hand, but she jerked away. He hung his head. "Your senses are getting better. I haven't fired a gun in weeks."

"Who are you, Seth?"

"You know me. We've hung out all summer."

Rylie's eyes narrowed. "Yeah? Something funny happened at the dance. One of the counselors told me that there is no camper named Seth. I wonder why he would think that?" She looked at him expectantly, but his expression didn't change. "You aren't from Camp Golden Lake."

"No, I'm not," Seth said.

Rylie took a deep breath, bracing herself for the logical leap from there. "You're the werewolf, aren't you?"

He laughed, and Rylie felt her heart sink into her stomach. She hadn't made the accusation thinking he would admit to it. When he saw her expression, he stopped laughing and quickly said, "No. I'm not a werewolf."

"Then who are you?"

"I'm a... well, I'm kind of a hunter," Seth said. "I hunt werewolves."

She gaped. "Does that mean... are you going to...?"

"You're not a werewolf yet. Not for one more moon." He took Rylie's hand in his, and this time, she didn't pull away. His skin was warm and rough. "You don't have to turn. You can fight it. If you can keep yourself from changing on the last moon by force of will, you'll never become a werewolf, and I won't have to..." He trailed off, leaving the rest unspoken.

"Kill me?" Rylie asked. He didn't respond.

"We both know there's a werewolf here. A real monster, not like you." Seth took a small cylinder out of a pocket on his cargo pants. It was the size of his thumb and shiny. A silver bullet. "When I find it, I'm going to kill it."

A heavy weight settled in her stomach. "What will you do to me?"

"You need to trust me, and you need to fight harder than you've ever fought in your life. I've seen the first transformation before. It's hard. When the moon rises, the curse will take you, and it's overwhelming. But if you're strong enough, you'll stay human."

"How do you know?" Rylie asked.

His face was very serious. "My brother was bitten on a hunt last year. He almost changed, but he didn't. He's fine now. Human."

She was silent for a long time, processing this new information while his thumb rubbed tiny circles over her knuckle. Rylie thought nothing could shock her anymore. The Legends had mentioned a few hunters, so it was no surprise people went out of their way to kill her kind.

But why did one of the hunters have to be *Seth*?

Rylie retracted her hand from his. "So that's where you got all your information. You know all about werewolves because you kill them." She swallowed. "You kill *us*. How many have you hunted before?"

"You don't want to know," Seth said.

She got off the bed and paced the cabin. He watched her move back and forth.

"Why would you try to be my friend if you knew you were going to hunt me down, too?" Rylie asked.

"It's hard to explain."

"Give it a try."

"I guess... well, I was there that night. When you were attacked. I tried to stop the werewolf, but I didn't make it in time. I had tracked it to that thicket of trees. I wanted to help you, but it was too fast."

"Is that why I survived?"

"Yeah," he said. "Maybe I should have let you die. You wouldn't have had to do any of this."

She grimaced. "Do you really think death is better?"

Instead of answering, he went on. "I wounded it, but I didn't kill it. You healed as soon as the attack ended, so I knew you had the curse. My brother would have killed you then and there, but I was weak. I didn't do it. I carried you back to your cabin instead," Seth said. "I didn't think..."

"That I would be weak, too? That I would kill Amber?" Rylie demanded.

"That I would care about you this much," he finished.

Her heart skipped a beat. "Oh."

"Amber wasn't your fault. You couldn't have done it. I lost track of you after you crossed the trail, and I know you didn't double back."

She didn't hear any of that. "You care about me?" Rylie asked, feeling light-headed.

Seth started to reach a hand toward her again, but seemed to think better of it. "Forget about it. I was too late to save you that night, but it's not too late to stop the change now. I swear I will do everything in my power to save you, Rylie."

"Is this why you wouldn't kiss me at the dance? You don't want to have to kiss me and then kill me?"

He stood, taking her by the shoulders. "Rylie…"

She drew back her hand and slapped him as hard as she could across the face. As it turned out, Rylie could hit really hard now. Seth's head snapped to the side. He staggered and barely caught himself on the wall of the cabin.

He wiped the back of his hand over his mouth. There was blood on it.

"Careful," he warned. "I won't let you do that again."

"I want you out of my sight. Now!"

"What will you do? Bite me?" Seth lifted his hands, palms out, in the universal gesture of peace. "You have to fight the anger, Rylie. That's not you. That's the beast." He took a step toward her. "Fight it!"

"I said you need to leave, and I meant it," Rylie said, fists clenched at her sides.

"Do you even want to live if it means being a werewolf? I wouldn't. You experienced the attack yourself. They're animals! The fact you survived is a miracle, because most people end up like Amber. Do you want to do that? Do you want to become a murderer?"

"I didn't say that! God, what kind of person do you think I am?"

"I don't know," he said. "What kind of person are you?"

She folded her arms to keep herself from lashing out again. "Why did you come here tonight? I know you're not going to apologize."

"No. I guess I'm not."

"Is this some kind of bargaining? You want to give me the choice between becoming a werewolf or... what, a mercy killing?"

"It would be a mercy," Seth said softly. "You don't want to live like that."

Rylie grit her teeth. "You don't know me."

"I know you better than anyone, Rylie."

Anger swelled within her again, but Rylie struck the side table instead of Seth. It shattered with a crack and her belongings spilled across the floor. He took a step back before be caught himself and straightened his shoulders.

Rylie's eyes narrowed. Showing a glimpse of weakness had been a bad idea. It made the wolf want to pounce. "I'm not going to let you kill me," she growled.

"Werewolves are dangerous. Worse, they're contagious. I've spent my whole life hunting with my family, and there aren't many packs left. This remnant is one of the last, and one of the worst. Tons of kids come through these camps. How many more could die, or end up like you?"

"I don't have to be like the one who changed me. If I didn't kill Amber—and I *really* hated her—I won't kill anyone," Rylie said. "Would you still hunt me?"

"My family is sworn to end the werewolf threat," Seth said.

"Including me."

It took him a long time to respond, but eventually, he nodded. "If you change tomorrow, then yes. Including you."

"Get out of my sight," Rylie spat.

He didn't argue this time. "Fine. I'll go. But you have to fight it, Rylie. You *have* to. Don't make me do anything I don't want to do."

She stepped up to him and jabbed a finger in his chest.

"You listen to me closely, Seth. I'm not making you do anything. If I change tomorrow night and you pull the trigger, then it will be *you* who killed me. Not your family. Not me. You." Rylie's chin trembled despite herself, and her voice softened. "Can you really kill me?"

Seth reached up and brushed his hand over her cheek. For once, all his emotions played out on his face simultaneously: fear, anger, betrayal, and maybe even love.

He took a long, shaking breath. "Goodbye, Rylie," he whispered. She didn't watch him leave. Rylie couldn't see him without getting angrier, and she didn't want to strike him again.

The only way she knew he was gone was because she suddenly felt empty and lonely. Rylie's eyes stung. Why was the only one who cared for her anymore sworn to kill her?

And why couldn't she help but love him back?

Eighteen

Attack on Camp Silver Brook

The new moon was going to rise that night, and Rylie was alone.

She didn't bother waiting for lights out before going up the mountain. As soon as Rylie filled herself on meat at breakfast, she took off at a run, making sure nobody could keep up with her. She had more food in her backpack, but Rylie was too fast for any normal human to follow even weighed down.

It didn't matter if anyone knew she was gone. How could they punish her now? The summer was at its end, and so was Rylie.

Once she was far enough from camp to be sure nobody would follow, Rylie slowed to a more reasonable pace. On any other day, it might have been a nice hike. The sun shone hot, but a light breeze cooled her sweat. The air became crisper the higher she climbed.

She walked on instinct, heading for a destination even she didn't know. It was as though something drew her higher and higher.

Rylie passed the ruins of the old church in the afternoon and stopped for lunch, hopping over the barbed wire and sitting on the stone pew inside. She ate ravenously, but tried to reserve most of her food for dinner that night.

The church wasn't as scary during the day. Rylie stared mistrustfully at the metal rings embedded in the wall. Somehow, knowing she had let a werewolf hunter—even Seth—chain her during a moon made her feel sick inside. She had been helpless. What if he had decided not to give her the chance to avoid the transformation and killed her?

Of course, Seth had ignored many opportunities to kill her: the first night she was bitten, every time he came to her cabin while she slept, when she was weak during her transformations. He hadn't done it yet.

"Yet" being the important word.

The pancakes were suddenly too dry in Rylie's mouth, so she put the rest of her supplies in her backpack.

Rylie decided to stay at the ruined outpost. It was as good a place as any. She was far from the camps, preventing a repeat of the Amber incident, and she had a clear view of the sky. She would be able to see the change coming.

As the sun inched across the sky and made the shadows lengthen, Rylie felt the moon begin to tug at her. It was different this time. Her nerves were jittered. At first, she thought she was only nervous, but it only got worse as time passed.

The change was going to be bad. Very bad.

Rylie pulled out her journal to pass the time, sipping from a water bottle as she wrote.

The hours passed as she told her story. Even though she had logged everything as it happened, she felt like she had to go over it one more time. She talked about her alienation at the beginning of summer and meeting Cassidy. She wrote about how much she missed her dad, and how she had grown to love the forest.

But mostly, she wrote about Seth.

She reached their argument the night before and stopped. Rylie didn't want to think about that.

Tonight's the night. It's my only chance to save myself. I have to be strong, like Seth said, but I don't know how. I'm scared.

He might be right. If I do change, I'm probably better off dead. I won't be able to go home. I don't even have a home anymore. Going back to the city for school is out of the question, especially since even my friends think I'm a freak by now.

I'm not the same person anymore. I don't want to die, diary, but I feel like I've reached the end of days anyway.

She sighed and kicked a piece of rubble across the church.

I wish Seth was here.

It grew too dark for Rylie to see the page. She chewed on the end of her pen, trying to decide how to finish the entry with the knowledge she might never write in it again. Her fingers traced over the deep scratch on the leather cover that had been left by her attacker three months ago. It felt like a lifetime.

I'm sorry I was bitten and that I'm becoming something evil. I guess it's good my dad didn't live to see this. But I promise if I survive the change, I'm really going to live. I'm not going to waste a single day.

I don't regret anything.

And she signed her name at the bottom. *Rylie.*

She shut the journal and tucked it in her bag to wait for sunset.

The forest darkened. Tendrils of orange and red clouds reached across the sky. Rylie tried to keep picking at her food, knowing she would regret it if she didn't eat, but she had no appetite. She forced herself to swallow down the ham and bacon, tossing the remaining pancakes to the squirrels. They wouldn't approach her to eat them. She really was alone.

Before long, the sun was gone, and the stars faded into place. Rylie stood in the middle of the encampment. She kept her ears perked, half-hoping to hear Seth coming for her, but it was quiet on Gray Mountain. All the small animals of the forest had gone to sleep.

Everything else was silent, as though watching her and waiting to see what would happen.

The moon would call her soon. Rylie could feel it.

"What am I going to do?" she asked the sky.

"I don't know, Rylie. What *are* you going to do?"

She spun. For a half-instant, she thought it was Seth, but then she saw the figure lumber across the ruined outpost. She knew those broad shoulders, that yellow hair, and those angry eyes. He was wearing khakis and a loose t-shirt branded with the camp's logo, and he carried nothing despite the long hike.

"Jericho," Rylie said, disappointed. "What do you want?"

"It's dangerous to be in the forest alone at night," he said.

"So what? Are you going to report me for being out past curfew?" she asked. The situation was almost funny. Here she was, an hour at most away from becoming a terrifying beast, and a camp counselor was trying to menace her.

"It's an option." He took a step forward, and she stood her ground. "But what good would that do?"

Rylie glanced up at the sky. The sun was completely gone. "If I promise I'll be back in bed by sunrise, will you leave me alone? You can't threaten me with anything and I'm not going back tonight."

Jericho laughed. "Neither am I."

There was a strange tone to his voice, and Rylie gave him a second, harder look. His eyes were almost reflective in the darkness.

She took a slow sniff of the air. The wind wasn't blowing in the right direction, and she wasn't as sensitive in human form, but she could almost pick up that musky, woodsy scent she had detected at Golden Lake. The same scent she had tracked on the last moon.

The scent of the werewolf.

"Oh my God," she whispered.

Jericho, already massive and intimidating, only seemed to grow bigger. He flashed sharp, white teeth. "Now you know."

"You're going to kill me, aren't you?"

"No, I'm not."

That gave her pause. "But…"

"You're just a pup," Jericho said. "I've come because it's your sixth moon. The first real transformation can be terrifying if you're alone. Why don't you let me help you tonight?"

"Help me? How?" Rylie asked.

"Join me. We can bring the werewolf population back to power if we work together. I know you've been spending time with the boy who has hunted me all summer—that Seth you mentioned. I only realized he had found you a few days ago."

"He's been helping me."

"Don't be confused. Those hunters are ruthless," Jericho said. "They've spent years wiping us out. He's been using you to get to me because he knew I would come back for you. I always do. I take care of my pack."

Rylie clenched her fists. "That's not true. Seth wouldn't do that."

"I've been trying to keep you out of trouble. I made sure you weren't kicked out of camp." Jericho tried to smile, but it didn't look as friendly as it was meant to be. "Aren't you scared, Rylie? Don't you want help?"

"No," she said, but she faltered inside. She did want help. She didn't want to fight the change alone, and if she did transform, she wanted someone to make sure nobody got hurt. But Rylie had imagined Seth helping her, not the man who mauled her. "What do you mean when you say you're going to restore the werewolf population?"

"It isn't a coincidence you survived that first night. We need to reproduce to survive against the threat of hunters. Camps Golden Lake and Silver Brook are a perfect opportunity! All those young, strong, healthy people are just waiting to be turned. It's not too late for our kind to thrive."

"You mean you're going on a killing spree?"

"They can't transform if they don't survive," Jericho said. "I want as many survivors as possible. The only ones who need to die are the hunters."

"But Amber…"

"She was an accident. She wasn't as strong as you."

She felt sick. He was proposing that they subject all the other campers to the trauma Rylie had suffered all summer. And many of them would die, just like Amber.

"No," she whispered.

"What?"

Rylie repeated herself more loudly this time. "No! I won't do it. It's wrong."

"You're going to betray your pack?"

"I don't have a pack," Rylie said. "If you want to help me, why didn't you come on an earlier moon? Why didn't you help when I was scared and confused and needed it the most? Maybe Seth is out to kill us, but you've got plenty of blood on your hands, too. At least he's been there for me."

He glanced up at the moon. "Fine. I don't have time to change your mind."

Rylie was strong, but Jericho had years of transformations on his side. He was much, much stronger.

He backhanded her. Pain exploded in Rylie's head.

Reeling from his first hit, she didn't see him coming for her a second time. He threw her into the wall of the ruined church. The stones cracked at the impact. She cried out and toppled to the ground as the stones crashed around her.

She threw her arms over her head to protect herself from falling rocks. Bricks thudded to the dirt and struck her shoulder.

"If that's your decision, then fine," Jericho said. "Just don't interfere."

Dropping to a crouch, Jericho ran away. He was as fast as he was strong. The last thing Rylie saw before he disappeared was his skin rippling and growing fur as he flung his shirt aside.

She groaned. Her shoulder was bleeding and it felt like her ribs were shattered.

Somehow, the injuries were far less frightening than Jericho's plan. He was going to try to bite all the campers. There was no question about it: most of them would die. The ones that didn't would become just like her.

It was wrong. Rylie couldn't let it happen.

She tried to ignore the pain, but it was easier said than done. Every beat of her heart sent blood rushing through the injuries, making them throb. That overwhelming heat began to rise within her, and she recognized the signs of her body healing itself.

Rylie shoved the stones off of her and got to her hands and knees. She couldn't wait to heal. She had to get to camp. She needed to warn everyone they were in danger.

She could only pray that she wasn't already too late.

Rylie stumbled into the campsite as her injuries continued to knit. It was easier to breathe with every footstep. Her bruises and cuts were mended, so her ribs wouldn't be far behind.

She heard crying before she could see the camp.

"Oh my God, oh my God!" someone wailed.

Shoving through the trees, Rylie emerged into the ring of cabins that had once been her campsite.

Jericho had already passed through. The benches around the campfire were destroyed. The door to Rylie's former cabin was in pieces, and when she peered in, she saw bloody smears on the floor as though someone had been dragged out.

The crying came from underneath the steps. Rylie knelt at the end to peer underneath, and the other girl screamed.

"Don't hurt me!"

It was Patricia, and she was a mess. Her mascara streamed down her cheeks, and her knees were filthy. But she wasn't hurt. The blood didn't belong to her.

"Shut up, it's me!" Rylie said.

Patricia kept screaming. Rylie rolled her eyes and reached under the steps to grab her by the shirt. She dragged her out one-handed. Patricia struggled, kicking and flailing with her fists. After Jericho's blows, they felt like gentle taps.

Rylie shook her by the shoulders. "I *told* you to shut up!"

Patricia finally opened her eyes and fell silent. "Rylie?"

"What happened? Has a wolf been through here?"

She nodded, and tears began rolling down her cheeks. "That—that thing—it killed… oh my God, it killed…" Patricia started wailing again.

"Where's everyone else?"

"They're gathered in the recreation hall. They found another one of the counselors dead, so they're organizing to evacuate. We were going to join them…"

"We? Who is 'we'?" Rylie asked. Patricia raised a trembling finger and pointed at a dark lump lying on the ground. "Get to the mess hall. Hurry!"

Rylie released her and Patricia fled. She dropped to her knees beside the body. It was too much of a mess to make out the face, but Rylie recognized the clothing and the whistle around her neck.

It was Louise.

She felt numb inside. Louise hadn't deserved to die. She had been one of the only ones at camp to be nice to her. For some reason, the only thing Rylie could think was, *She ordered tofu for me.* It raced through her mind over and over.

She ordered tofu for me...

A scream pierced the air. Rylie left the body behind and ran toward the office. There was nothing she could do for Louise anymore.

Girls were scattered through the main camp, trying to reach the recreation hall. Jericho was there. He was almost the size of a horse, with thick, shaggy fur stained by blood. Saliva dribbled from his jaw.

When he saw her, his mouth fell open in a wolfish grin. Rylie's heart raced. He was happy to see her because she would be uncontrollable if she changed in the camp, and she would surely attack someone. That couldn't happen.

He leaped toward one of the last girls lingering outside, silver claws digging deep furrows in the earth.

Rylie jumped at the same time.

She knocked into the camper's side. They both fell as Jericho rushed overhead. He landed several feet away.

"Go!" she shouted, and the camper scrambled to her feet.

He spun on Rylie with a growl, lip curled back. His fangs were bright and shiny, and Rylie wondered if he had killed Louise on purpose. The two counselors had been friends. Anger clenched in her chest like a fist, leaving no room for fear.

Rylie felt her own wolf rise within her, flushing her skin and making her hair stand on end. *Louise.* He had killed Louise.

"You want to eat someone, Jericho? You eat me!" she shouted.

He seemed to consider it, and even took a step toward her. Rylie didn't flinch. If he was going to kill her, so be it—but she would go down fighting, not crying.

Shots rang out.

Jericho didn't stop to see where they came from. He bounded into the forest immediately, so fast he was barely more than a blur.

He wasn't gone. Rylie could smell him close.

She turned to search for the source of the shots. Seth stood on the top row of the concrete amphitheater around the campfire, lowering his rifle. His eyes lit when he saw her. "Rylie!"

"Seth!"

She ran to him and grabbed his hand. Seth looked more like a soldier than the boy she had come to know. He wore a black shirt and pants that were armored with material she could only assume was resistant to werewolf bites. The long, wicked belt knife hung at his waist again.

"Are you okay? What happened?" he asked, touching her lower lip. She hadn't realized she had been bleeding. The injury was already gone.

"I ran into the werewolf. It's Jericho, the counselor on the other side. Everyone is gathering in the recreation hall. He must know that. If he gets in there, it will be a blood bath!"

Seth's jaw clenched. "Jericho. Okay, you need to get somewhere safe. Is the moon calling yet?" She shook her head. "It takes awhile the first time. Get inside somewhere. Somewhere *alone.* It will be easier if you can't see the sky."

"Where are you going?" Rylie asked.

"Hunting," he said. Seth looked conflicted. "Look…" He searched for words without coming up with anything, mouth moving soundlessly.

"What?"

He grabbed both of her shoulders and kissed her hard.

Rylie wished desperately for time to stop so she could enjoy the moment. A hurried kiss while the camp fell apart under werewolf attack wasn't how she hoped her first kiss with Seth would happen. She thought there would be a lot more heart pounding and swooning and promises of love. All she could do was cling to him and try to catch her breath when he released her.

"I should have done that ages ago," he said.

"Seth…"

"The moon is rising," Seth said urgently, searching her eyes. "Fight it, Rylie. *Please.* One werewolf has to die tonight. I don't want it to be two."

He dropped her shoulders and ran off. There was a bag hanging from his belt that was probably loaded with silver bullets.

And one of them might have her name on it.

"Be careful," Rylie whispered.

Nineteen

Moon Called

Where could she go?

Rylie looked around the camp. The recreation would have been best, since it was a big, empty room with metal doors. But now everybody was piling tables against the windows in there, forming a barricade.

The only other big building available was the mess hall. It would have to do. At least if Rylie got hungry, she would have plenty to eat.

Jericho's attack must have interrupted the cleaning staff. The doors to the mess hall were wide open, and soapy water was spilled across the floor. The mop was a few feet away in three pieces. Rylie kicked the bucket out of the way and pulled the doors shut behind her

Just before the door closed, Rylie caught sight of someone standing out in the camp. It was Cassidy. She was shuffling around in too-long jeans and picking at her black nail polish. With her keen eyesight, Rylie could see fresh drawings on her bare arms.

"Cassidy! Hey, Cassidy!"

She was too far away to hear. Hoping that the moon wouldn't call her too quickly, Rylie ran out to talk to her.

Cassidy looked up when Rylie approached. "Hey."

"What are you doing out here? Two of the counselors were killed! You have to get inside the rec hall," Rylie said.

"I'll get inside," Cassidy promised. "I'm just waiting for something."

"What?"

She pointed straight up. Rylie followed her finger to see a small, dark patch of sky. A few weeks earlier, she would have been clueless, but now she knew it was the new moon hiding amongst the stars. She could feel its pull tugging at her heart.

"I can't change on command yet, like Jericho," she said. "I've been changing earlier in the night, though."

Rylie stared. "*What?*"

"He didn't tell you that I'm like you two?"

"You're a *werewolf?*"

"Why do you think I went out of my way to make friends? I told you this was my second year at camp," Cassidy said. "Jericho got to me last year."

"I don't... I mean... When did he bite you? Did you choose it?"

A hint of pain flickered across her face. "No."

"Aren't you mad?"

"I was at first, but he's right. I'm a werewolf now, and I can't change that. But I can change the fact we're being slaughtered by hunters and kept as trophies. I can make it a better world for us to live in."

"It's wrong for hunters to kill werewolves, but it's just as wrong to attack all those people and change them against their will. Do you know how many of them will end up dead like Amber?" Rylie asked.

"Just the weak ones." Cassidy shrugged. "Who cares?"

"I do," she whispered.

"Then maybe you're one of the weak ones, too." She turned her face toward the sky, staring at the invisible moon.

A shiver rolled over her body. Rylie could see her skin ripple like water in a pond. "Guess it's time."

The change was horrifying to watch. Cassidy's jaw and nose burst forward as though they might tear out of her face. Her mouth spread in a long smile. Her teeth grew sharp and her ears became pointed. She screamed, and it sounded like any girl screaming at first—but then it turned into a howl, chilling and sharp in the cool night.

Rylie backed away slowly, hands covering her mouth. She didn't want to see it. She didn't want to know what was going to happen to her.

Cassidy got down on all fours before her knees snapped and reversed, pulling her shirt over her head with hands that quickly grew wicked claws. Her shredded jeans tore and fell to the ground as her body doubled in size. For a moment, she was a hideous, hairless wolf with a rat-like tail growing from her spine. Then shiny black fur erupted from her bubbling skin.

Unlike Rylie, who had been more human than animal on the last moon, Cassidy looked like a demon. Her eyes glowed red. Her teeth were jagged and sharp. She smelled rancid, like Jericho, but a thousand times worse.

Suddenly, Rylie recalled the last time she had turned. *Two werewolves.* Cassidy had been the smaller one all along. She remembered the wolf's bloody face.

Cassidy had killed Amber. It hadn't been Rylie at all.

Her momentary relief was quickly overwhelmed by fear. Cassidy had killed and she didn't seem to feel any remorse about it. Now she was staring at Rylie with glowing red eyes, and she looked hungry.

Words from The Legends of Gray Mountain came to mind: *In the early years, he is the most mindless, the hungriest, and he knows insatiable hunger.*

"Cassidy," Rylie said. "Don't hurt me."

She didn't show any signs of recognition.

Cassidy was gone.

Rylie ran.

She heard the giant wolf follow, claws scrabbling against the ground. Rylie found speed within her that she didn't know she had.

Trees flashed past. She let her animal instincts guide her rather than her conscious human mind.

Tremors began to spread over her limbs. The dark forest was trying to strip away her human flesh. Her heart beat faster as she ran harder, and her blood burned through her arteries.

She recognized the fever. The weakness.

The moon was calling her, too.

Cassidy yipped and growled as she chased. She was close.

Rylie was afraid, but the animal within was angry. The wolf wasn't prey. The wolf was a predator, and it was being challenged by another. It knew Cassidy. This wasn't the first time it had run from her, but it wanted it to be the last.

She swept a heavy branch off the ground and spun, swinging with all her might.

Crack! It connected with Cassidy's face.

The werewolf yelped and fell back. Rylie advanced on her, swinging again. Cassidy caught the branch in her jaws. She jerked it out of Rylie's hands and nearly pulled her off her feet.

Rylie dove toward the branch, but Cassidy got in her way. Her red eyes burned.

A twig cracked behind her. Cassidy looked away for just an instant, but it was long enough.

Rylie hauled a boulder off the ground. She shouldn't have been able to pick it up, but it felt as light as her school bag.

She smashed it into Cassidy's head.

The same fast healing that kept Rylie healthy and whole worked just as well for Cassidy. She recovered quickly and snapped at Rylie. Her jaws grazed her arm, shredding the skin.

"Stop it! You don't have to do this!" Rylie cried. The werewolf sniffed the air as though her pungent blood was enticing. She pressed a hand to the wound to try to stave the flow. "It's not too late, Cassidy. You don't have to be bad!"

It was a lie. Rylie knew it had been too late the instant Cassidy killed Amber. But it made her falter.

Rylie didn't give her the chance to think twice about it.

Jumping on Cassidy's back, Rylie wrapped her arms around the thick fur at her neck. The werewolf shrieked and bucked, twisting to bite at Rylie's legs. She shut her eyes and hung on as tightly as she could.

It was just like riding one of the friskier horses at her aunt's ranch. The thought was so absurd Rylie almost laughed.

Instead, she squeezed tighter, pressing her fists into Cassidy's trachea.

Cassidy's thrashing grew weaker. She staggered.

With a final burst of energy, Cassidy slammed her body sideways into the tree. Rylie couldn't hold on. Her hands slipped free.

The werewolf tore away from her, spinning with a growl. Her eyes were darker than before.

Rylie could see her death in them.

Scrambling to her feet, she tried to run again. Her foot caught on a root. Her ankle twisted and broke with a snap. Crying out, Rylie collapsed.

She tried to get up, but she wasn't fast enough.

Cassidy leapt.

A shot rang out.

Her body jerked in midair, then struck Rylie. It knocked them both to the ground. Rylie shrieked, anticipating the tearing pain of claws and teeth.

But Cassidy didn't attack once Rylie was flattened. She was a dead weight.

"Oh my God," Rylie whispered. "Oh my God."

She pushed the body off of her and slid out from underneath. Her ankle burned as the broken bones quickly knit. Her hands were bloodstained.

Seth stood at the edge of the clearing, his rifle aimed. He hurried forward and put himself between Rylie and Cassidy. The muzzle stayed trained on her skull the entire time in case she moved again, but Rylie knew it wasn't necessary. Seth's first bullet had done the job. Cassidy was dead.

"Are you okay?" he asked, reaching down to squeeze Rylie's hand.

"I'm alive." Her voice was shaking. She grasped her ankle between both hands as it burned and throbbed with supernatural healing.

He knelt by Cassidy's body, slinging his rifle over his shoulder. "It's smaller than I expected," Seth said with a frown. He held his hand up to her paw, spreading his fingers out to judge the size. "I'm sure I found bigger prints."

"This isn't the only one. She's not Jericho, he's…" A huge, hulking form rose behind Seth, and Rylie's eyes widened. "Seth! Behind you!"

He spun, but he couldn't raise his gun in time.

Jericho slammed into Seth, taking them both to the ground. Seth's head bounced on a rock. He gave a sharp cry and fell silent.

Rylie's heart skipped a beat. "No!"

Biting down on Seth's calf, Jericho turned at the sound. There was more intelligence in his eyes than there had been for Cassidy. She was nuts, but he knew exactly what he was doing. He was just as human as he was monster, and that was even more terrifying than the younger werewolf had been.

"Let him go," Rylie ordered, voice trembling. She got up, keeping her weight on her good ankle.

Jericho growled, baring his teeth around Seth's leg, and he backed away without dropping it.

It was a challenge. He was daring her to follow him, knowing that she wouldn't be able to take him on unless she was a wolf, too—and once she changed, she probably wouldn't *want* to fight him.

In the early years, he is the most mindless, the hungriest, and he knows insatiable hunger…

Rylie couldn't let Jericho take Seth. She moved to follow, but a strange feeling seized her when she stepped out of the shelter of the trees. It was a strong, low cramping in her chest and belly.

The transformation.

"No," she whispered.

As she watched, ripples ran down her skin and left goose bumps in their wake. It was like the fur was growing inside of her. It was fighting to push its way out.

Claws erupted from her fingertips, and Rylie shut her fists tight. She squeezed her eyes closed.

Focusing on her mental image of her own reflection—a leggy, pale girl with blonde hair and blue eyes, not gold like the wolf—she fought to concentrate on everything human.

Her clothes. The city. Her mom's condo. School.

When she opened her eyes again, her skin had stopped rippling.

She stared at her hands until her claws grew thin and became fingernails again.

Rylie forced herself to take deep even breaths. She wasn't going to become something evil. Seth wanted her to fight it, so she would.

Even if it left her helpless to save him.

Twenty

The Third Werewolf

Failure.

Rylie sat beneath the boulder, hugging her knees to her chest. She could feel the moon fighting against everything that made her human to free the beast inside. She shivered and poured sweat at the same time. Her teeth chattered. She dug her fingernails into her shins to keep holding on.

Seth was at Jericho's mercy. She was the only one who could save him, but she was a failure, crying helplessly in the darkness.

She forced herself to her feet and stumbled back to camp. Everyone was still locked in the recreation room. By the time she found the mess hall, she could barely see through the moon's haze clouding her vision.

Even though the moon was dark, it felt like she burst with its silver light. Rylie's veins pulsed with its fire. It pressed against her bones, straining against her muscles and fighting to break free of her flesh.

A wolf howled on the mountain. Jericho was taunting her. He wanted her to change.

"No," she whimpered through grit teeth. "*No.*"

Rylie was burning up. The fire was going to consume her.

She shut the door to the mess hall and wrapped her arms around her body. There was nothing she could do now but wait for morning.

And why not? Everyone was safe.

Everyone… except Seth.

"He's a werewolf hunter," she whispered to the darkened mess. "He would kill me. I shouldn't…" A spasm rocked her, and she groaned, shutting her eyes. "…I shouldn't even care about him."

But she did.

She dug her nails into the windowsill and pressed her forehead against the glass. It was Seth's voice that called to her from within. *Fight it…*

It was what he wanted. He didn't want her to risk herself by saving him. Rylie was just following his orders.

Fight it…

With her eyes shut, she could almost make out her dad's face. It was broad and friendly. He was smiling at her even though she was becoming something terrible.

What would he want her to do? Would he want her to hide when she could save someone's life?

Rylie remembered sitting with him on their porch swing the week before camp started. His arm was warm over her shoulders and they were sharing a bag of popcorn.

"You're strong, pumpkin," he told her, giving her shoulders a gentle squeeze. "Stronger than your mother and me combined. I need you to be brave this summer. It's only going to get harder before it gets better."

She had been angry at the time. How could she be brave when her world was falling apart? Rylie felt like she was losing her family, and it was the worst thing she could have imagined.

That was before Camp Silver Brook and the attack. Before she found out there were worse things to lose than her parent's marriage.

I need you to be brave.

He wouldn't have wanted Rylie to hide.

"I don't want to be evil, dad," she whispered.

He was replaced in her mind by Louise. Not the awful, mangled body she had seen earlier that night—the smiling counselor that reminded her of a gym teacher.

She recalled their conversation the night Rylie stole the keys to the SUV. *The werewolf thing—that was a deal between the humans and the animal gods. It was a blessing meant to bring man and nature together. It ended the war.*

Somehow, Rylie didn't think that Louise would have thought her to be evil.

But how could it be a blessing?

She considered the question. Being bitten by a werewolf had made her stronger. She wasn't the weak, whining thing she had been at the beginning of the summer. Three months of partial transformations might have been difficult, but it had also made her a better person. Rylie liked who she was becoming.

Maybe she wouldn't go home. She didn't want to anyway, since she couldn't go home to her dad or any of her friends, who had to know what happened at The South Den by now.

Rylie could move away and live alone using her father's money. She could make her own future.

And now Seth was in danger. Maybe he would hunt her, but maybe he wouldn't. It didn't change anything about the time they had spent together. He was a good person at the core—better than Jericho. Rylie loved him. It was crazy to love someone sworn to kill you, but she couldn't help it.

Seth wasn't just the only good thing about camp. He was the best thing left in her life.

He would die if she didn't intervene, and the only way she could save him was by embracing the wolf.

She opened the door and stepped into the night air, facing the peak where Jericho must have taken Seth. They would be at the top, at the temple where the animals communed with the gods. Rylie was sure of it.

"I'm going to save him," Rylie said. She wasn't sure who she wished could hear her—Seth, Louise, or her dad.

For the first time in weeks, she didn't feel alone.

Rylie stripped off her clothes and let go.

At first, it seemed like nothing would happen. All the muscles in her body relaxed. The piercing pain in her skull subsided.

Instead of the wolf fighting its way out, Rylie felt like her human self melted away, allowing the beast to emerge. The bones of her skull crunched and cracked. The skin stretched over her protruding jaw. Fur blossomed down her shoulders.

The mind of the animal came to the forefront, numbing the pain as her knees reversed and her spine elongated. *It's not as bad as you thought, Seth,* she wanted to say, but Rylie no longer had lips with which to speak.

She waited to disappear from herself and fade into the background of a wild mind as she had on every moon beforehand.

It didn't happen.

The wolf was there. It processed the overwhelming input from smells and sounds as it licked its paws and considered the human blood splashed on the ground. But Rylie was there, too. She thought the same thoughts and felt the same things.

It took her a moment to realize that Rylie and the wolf were one and the same. They weren't separate creatures at all.

She didn't have time to examine her new, full-wolf body, or how strong and hungry she felt. She couldn't fear for her humanity. She couldn't wonder what was going to happen to her on every moon to come. Rylie focused on the thing that had inspired her in the first place: Seth. She needed to save Seth.

Throwing back her head, she loosed a howl that she knew Jericho would hear.

I am coming.

The peak of the mountain was draped in darkness.

Seth struggled toward consciousness as he was dragged across the ground. His leg was in so much pain it had gone numb. His rifle dragged behind him by the shoulder strap, and dirt inched past his face. Mud smeared up his cheek and into his hair.

He tried to focus his bleary eyes. The haze of pain almost kept him from making out the massive teeth clamped on his leg and the feeling of immense pressure where jaws pressed his armor against him.

Seth was a few layers of fabric away from being cursed.

He reached for his gun. His head swam and his hands were clumsy, so he couldn't grip anything. Jericho pulled him onto a stone surface and released Seth's leg, then took the rifle in his mouth and tossed it aside.

"You should run," Seth mumbled. "I'm going to kill you."

He realized it didn't sound threatening, but he had to try. Jericho let out a cruel, laughing yip.

Shaking his head to clear it, Seth examined his surroundings. Stone pillars towered above him, forming a ring. There were no other mountains in sight. He was at the very top of Gray Mountain.

Seth had read all the legends from his family's books, but he never believed it was real, even though he spent half the summer looking for it.

The temple.

Jericho was even more intimidating as a wolf than as a human. His dark form silhouetted against the stars was like a black hole. A chill ran over Seth when he realized the werewolf was examining him. Jericho was trying to figure out why he hadn't torn through Seth's clothing.

But he wasn't attacking. He was waiting.

For what?

Jericho strolled away, staring at a starless patch of sky.

Seth wasn't safe yet. Just because Jericho hadn't bitten him didn't mean he wouldn't try. He searched the dark mountaintop for his rifle and saw it wedged between two boulders further down the slope.

He tested his legs by trying to get onto his knees. They wouldn't support his weight. Seth had sprained something—maybe even broken a few bones. But he needed his gun.

It was so quiet on the top of the mountain. All he could hear was the cold, gusting wind. His hands slipped on ice as he began to drag himself toward his rifle. Seth wasn't dressed for such high elevations. His fingers were losing sensation.

Jericho only needed two steps to cross the distance between them. He shoved Seth with his muzzle to keep him from the gun.

Seth shoved back, pushing his face away, but Jericho only nudged him again. It was like the werewolf was toying with him. "Are you waiting for Rylie?" Seth demanded, his breath fogging the air.

Jericho's head tilted to the side. His hot breath stank of rotten meat and his fur smelled like mud.

"She won't come," he went on. "She's too strong to transform."

The werewolf didn't react. Seth moved experimentally toward his gun again, but a heavy paw crushed his chest. Jericho's weight bore down on his ribcage and he gasped at the pressure. The message was clear: *Don't move.*

Jericho turned to stare at the moon again.

"She's not coming," Seth insisted.

He unhooked the knife from his belt. If he could just provoke Jericho into attacking, maybe he could get at his weak underbelly. It was his only chance. Seth wasn't ready to die.

"You were going to try to change everyone at camp, weren't you? Nobody you bit has survived and everyone else got to safety where you can't reach them. All you have left is Rylie, but she's not going to transform tonight." Seth could only pray it was true.

Jericho began to pace. Each time his paws hit the stone, it sounded like a sandbag falling. He had to have been the biggest werewolf Seth had ever seen.

"I killed your pup," Seth said. "You're alone now, and nobody will ever come back to these camps. You failed."

Jericho finally returned his attention to Seth. His teeth were bared and his hackles rose as he stalked toward the hunter. Seth flipped the knife around in his hand and braced himself for the attack.

But it never came.

A second dark shape appeared on one of the highest pillars, gazing down at them. Its fur glowed gold in the starlight.

Seth's heart plummeted into his gut.

Rylie.

The two werewolves studied each other from a distance. Jericho's fur smoothed and his tail swished once. He gave an inquiring yip, as though to ask if she was on his side. It was almost a sad sound. Seth wondered if he was upset about losing his pup.

He held his breath waiting for Rylie's response. Jericho yipped again. Rylie growled, and Jericho's fur stood on end.

She leaped down. The wolves collided like two fronts of a storm.

Rylie landed on Jericho's back, and her claws raked red stripes down his spine. He freed himself of her in a flash. They didn't play around—they were both out for blood.

They crashed together. Jericho's teeth tore at Rylie's ear. She buried her claws in his belly. They rolled and fell, hitting the rocks below.

Seth didn't stop to watch. He hurried toward his rifle, dragging himself as quickly as he could across the slick ground with a lame leg. Every little motion sent pain rippling anew through his body, but there was nothing more motivational than knowing he was stranded alone with two bloodthirsty animals.

A furred body tumbled past him. Seth couldn't tell which one it was. He buried his knife in it, and the responding howl was deeper than Rylie's growls. Jericho jerked the knife out of Seth's hand, the blade trapped between his ribs.

The werewolf barely noticed it. He hurtled toward Rylie again, limping slightly on one side.

She leaped onto one of the pillars, and then to another. Jericho followed.

Seth's freezing fingers wrapped around the barrel of his rifle, and he pulled it out of the rocks. It was banged up from having been thrown aside. He fumbled for the silver cartridges in his pocket.

A strangled scream reached Seth. He knew he shouldn't have been afraid for Rylie—it was too late for her now—but he felt sick to see Jericho's jaws buried in her throat. Her cries were strangled and raw.

Having her windpipe torn open barely phased her. Jericho was older and stronger, but Rylie had all the fury and energy of a new werewolf on her side.

She jerked free and snapped at the side of his face.

Seth's fingers trembled as he loaded the bullets into the bottom of his rifle. He needed at least two rounds. He didn't want to think of how he needed to use them.

He raised the barrel to aim. They were atop the pillars now. Too far away to hit. Seth held it steady, waiting for them to come closer.

Rylie tore into Jericho's belly, and his head swung around to bite her. He was losing blood. Sluggish. She had all but gutted him.

It was almost too awful to watch. Jericho staggered. He nipped at her remaining ear, but the fresh blood was quickly lost amongst everything around Rylie's throat. They wavered atop the rocks, two silhouettes at a standstill against the stars.

With a final burst of energy, Rylie jumped forward and knocked into his side.

Jericho tumbled off the pillar of rock and landed on the slope near Seth with a sick *crunch*.

Dropping down, Rylie stumbled and barely caught herself. Her teeth were bared for another bite—but Jericho's back was twisted at a strange angle. His mouth hung open and there was nothing in his eyes. His forepaw twitched once.

Seth fired from his position on the ground. The slug buried in the wolf's carcass, but Jericho didn't react.

She had killed him. Rylie had killed Jericho.

Seth stared between the two werewolves. Rylie dipped her head to sniff the body and licked her nose as though to taste his odors. The fur over her shoulders smoothed.

He fired a second time. Rylie flinched, but this shot wasn't aimed at her, either. Seth hit Jericho again to make *really* sure he was dead. He would take no chances with an animal that big.

Now that adrenaline was fading, Seth's twisted leg throbbed. He couldn't shake the memory of being dragged through the forest like a prize.

Rylie turned her stare from Jericho to Seth.

She took a step forward, and he tried to get to his feet again, but his leg collapsed under him. He sat down hard.

Seth leveled his rifle at Rylie. He stared at her down the barrel, meeting her reflective golden gaze. She was a beautiful wolf, much more slender than Jericho, and more catlike than the one Seth killed earlier. Her shaggy mane was golden blonde and matted at the throat where Jericho had torn into her.

Something in her eyes was human. She recognized him. Her lip curled over her fangs.

He tried to get onto his knees so he could brace himself better, but it was hard to balance on one leg. And now he was starting to freeze. Seth could barely move. If she attacked, he wouldn't be able to get away.

His finger tensed on the trigger, but he didn't squeeze even though every instinct told him he should.

Seth could end the horrors of Gray Mountain if he killed her. She wasn't Rylie anymore. The wolf had taken her, and she was evil now.

But still, he didn't fire.

"I'm sorry," he whispered.

Rylie lowered her head and her lips slid back over her sharp teeth.

She turned and limped down the rocky slope toward the trees. Her left leg was mangled, and blood dripped onto the rocks from her throat.

Her back faced him. It was time to shoot.

But she hadn't attacked him. Seth couldn't pull the trigger. She wasn't just a werewolf, after all—she was *Rylie*.

Seth lowered his gun. Rylie disappeared into the darkness.

Epilogue

The Day After

Seth's brother called him early the next morning.

"Did you finally do it?" Abel asked.

"Yeah. I killed the werewolf and his pup," Seth said, using an earpiece so he had both hands free for packing up his camp. He loaded his rifle onto his motorcycle and checked the straps to make sure it fit snugly.

"Awesome. My bike better be in one piece, unlike the last solo hunt."

Seth snorted. "Your baby is fine."

"Better be," Abel said. He wasn't mad. He sounded proud.

Once his saddlebags were packed with the last of his clothing and supplies, Seth limped over to his squat tent and pulled up the stakes. After sleeping on the hard ground for three months, he was eager to get home, and the sorry state of his leg didn't help. Even though Seth had made a rough splint from a sturdy branch and bandages, he needed to get to a doctor soon if he wanted to preserve his ability to walk.

"How are you feeling?" Seth asked. Abel had avoided transforming on his sixth moon after being bitten—unlike

Rylie—but it was still a struggle every time the moon went full or new. It was a long, slow road to recovery.

"As good as can be expected." He suddenly sounded exhausted. "Mom helped."

"Sorry, man," Seth said.

Pulling on a helmet, he rode down the trail to the mouth of camp. He kept to the side to avoid hikers and cars, but there weren't any people left to avoid. He didn't cross paths with anyone on his way down the mountain.

Abel cleared his throat. "How was the hunt?"

Seth paused on the motorcycle, planting a foot on the ground to maintain his balance. He looked back over his shoulder to the forest he was leaving behind. Both camps had been emptied out within hours of sunrise, and nobody seemed sure if they would ever reopen.

Once he splinted his leg, Seth had spent the day cleaning up the werewolves' bodies and searching for Rylie. He kept looking until darkness fell again. He wasn't the only one on Gray Mountain. Rangers were still looking for Jericho, Cassidy, and Rylie, all of whom were considered "missing."

Seth found no signs of her. Most werewolves left telltale marks on their first moon, like dozens of dead animals, destroyed trees, and a bloodstain where they transformed. They could sleep for days after the first real change, so she should have been easy to locate.

Rylie left nothing behind.

He had, however, found a backpack in the ruins of the old outpost. Most of it was uninteresting. He didn't care about the sandwiches, half-empty water bottle, or the trail mix. But there had been one thing of note: Rylie's journal. He had it in his saddlebags now. He wasn't sure if he would ever read it.

He wanted to believe the werewolf hadn't taken over, but he feared that the alternative wasn't much better. Rylie's throat had been torn out by Jericho. There was a very good chance she hadn't survived.

Seth didn't know what he would have done if he found Rylie anyway. While his family didn't kill werewolves in human form, they wouldn't welcome her with open arms. He missed his chance to shoot her as a wolf. He wouldn't be able to do it if he came across her again.

Maybe it didn't matter. They never would have worked out. Hunter and hunted—their relationship was doomed from the start.

Seth never should have let himself fall in love with her.

It took him too long to realize Abel was still talking. "Do you hear me, Seth? I asked how your hunt went."

"Fine," Seth finally said. "It went fine."

Kicking off, he tore down the trail with a cloud of dust in his wake. The camps were empty and silent, as though in mourning for what happened the night before. Even all the animals seemed to have abandoned Gray Mountain.

Distantly, somewhere beyond the lake, a mournful howl rose amongst the trees.

About the Author

SM Reine is a writer and graphic designer obsessed with werewolves, the occult, and collecting swords. Sara spins tales of dark fantasy to escape the drudgery of the desert, where she lives with her husband, the Helpful Baby, and a small army of black familiars.

Sign up to be notified of new releases
and get a free ebook!
eepurl.com/eWERY

CPSIA information can be obtained at www.ICGtesting.com
Printed in the USA
LVOW13s1616080814

398214LV00022B/1057/P